DRAGON'S BELLE

MAGIC, FUR AND CLAWS
BOOK 2

EVE LANGLAIS

Copyright © 2023/2024 Eve Langlais

Cover art by © Atra Luna's Book Cover and Logo Art

Produced in Canada

Published by Eve Langlais

http://www.EveLanglais.com

Ebook ISBN: 978 177 384 4480

Print ISBN: 978 177 384 449 7

ALL RIGHTS RESERVED

This books is a work of fiction and the characters, events and dialogue found within the story are of the author's imagination and are not to be construed as real. Any resemblance to actual events or persons, either living or deceased, is completely coincidental.

No part of this book may be reproduced or shared in any form or by any means, electronic or mechanical, including but not limited to digital copying, file sharing, audio recording, email and printing without permission in writing from the author.

INTRODUCTION

DRAGONS AND WITCHES AREN'T SUPPOSED TO MIX, BUT LOVE DOESN'T CARE.

Clarabelle's been tasked by her coven to look into the disappearance of some witches. During the course of her investigation, she saves a man.

Not just any man, a dragon.

Dracin can't believe that, in his most embarrassing moment, he is rescued by a woman his beast insists is their mate. A tiny but fiery witch who makes him want more than his lonely existence.

Love should be simple, but between a coven that strongly disapproves and vampires determined to harm them, they'll have to fight for their happily ever after.

Look for more witch and shifter romance? Check out my website at EveLanglais.com

1

"On to the next order of business. Changing our broom supplier."

A very bored Clarabelle wanted to scream. The quarterly Colony Coven meeting was tedious, as usual. At times, Clarabelle wondered if she'd gotten stuck in a witchy version of *Groundhog Day*. Without even trying, she could have predicted the subjects they would cover, because they never seemed to change much.

First on the agenda, dwindling recruitment numbers. Today's witches lacked interest in joining a coven with restrictive rules, even though those laws were in place for their protection. Not even the temptation of real power could draw them in. Gone were the days when most witches worshipped the Lord of Hades. Now, new wave, crystal-loving wannabe witches fell in with the Wiccans, who had been making a comeback.

Item two on the quarterly docket, the All Hallows'

Eve committee needed volunteers to ensure the yearly bonfire and ensuing orgy with Satan went smoothly. The Dark Lord did so hate it when he didn't get at least one virgin to deflower. Never mind the fact that, in these modern times, virgins who made it to adulthood were a rarity.

Three, the coven coffers could use some replenishing. Bribing officials to look the other way when they almost burned down the forest didn't come cheap. It didn't matter the bonfire happened on private land. Eco warriors had been trying to get their old and sacred forest declared a historical site, complete with a permanent fire ban put in place.

Which led to number four, should they be hexing those annoying climate change twats? Bonfires weren't their only target. They had a long list of causes they fought for that would affect the coven's way of life. No witch wanted to see their gas stove banned. Cauldron cooking on an electric range just didn't work the same.

Five—

"Are we boring you, Clarabelle?" The rebuke from Marjorie, current Coven Witch Superior dragged her attention back to the meeting at hand.

"Uh, sorry. Just thinking of the ride home. Forecast says rain." She'd not checked before leaving on her broom.

"Afraid you'll melt like your great-aunt?" mocked Jezebel. Then mimicked the famous line from the movie in a high-pitched voice, "I'm melting!"

"You know it was a badly cast rain-repelling spell

that caused my aunt to die most horribly," Clarabelle stated primly. "And you shouldn't talk. With the amount of makeup you're wearing, once you get wet, you'll be lucky if you're not mistaken for a ghoul."

"Why you—"

"Daughters, that's quite enough." Marjorie's firm tone quieted them both.

Clarabelle could have kicked herself for rising to Jezebel's bait. "Sorry, Witch Superior," she mumbled, even as she plotted revenge on Jezebel. The kind that couldn't be traced to her. Their rivalry began in college and never stopped. Perhaps a hex on Jezebel's favorite mascara? She'd read about one that turned eyelashes into wiggling spider legs.

"Seeing as how these meetings bore you, I have a task you can concentrate on. Two actually. Jezebel, you'll be travelling to New York for Comicon with the aim of recruiting prospects."

"Me? Why not her?" Jezebel jabbed a finger at Clarabelle.

"Because she is going to be investigating the suspicious disappearances of some witches in Ottawa, Canada."

"Canada, as in the frozen wasteland north of us?" Jezebel snickered, whereas Clarabelle held in a sigh. She wasn't about to point out that Ottawa pretty much had the same weather as New York because she didn't want to piss off Marjorie, given the task sounded interesting. She'd not done anything of any note in months unless a pregnant hippo—by a drunk ogre—counted.

He'd claimed he thought it was his wife. Said wife got offended seeing as how her girth was at least double that of the pregnant zoo animal.

Marjorie didn't let Jezebel's taunting pass. "Maybe you're not the best person to send given your ignorance of simple geography. Do better or the next time you open your mouth to bray something stupid, I'll turn you into a donkey."

Ouch.

With that rebuke, the meeting ended, but Marjorie signaled for Clarabelle to remain behind.

She slid a folder over to Clarabelle, saying, "I didn't want to say anything in front of the rest of the coven, but you should know there might be danger."

"You think the disappearances are linked to foul play?"

"It seems most likely, seeing as how it's not just witches reported missing. We also have received reports of numerous werewolves losing touch with the local pack, as well as a half-elf, and a gargoyle. And those are just the ones we know of."

"We're sure they didn't relocate?" Clarabelle questioned.

"Without taking a single thing with them?"

"Any clues as to why anyone would want to harm or take them?"

Marjorie shrugged. "Your guess is as good as mine. I mean, if this were the Dark Ages, I'd suspect witch hunters, but with the wolves and others... It could be anything."

"You don't think it's the government, do you?" A fear held by non-humans everywhere. It didn't help that Hollywood movies and shows like *Stranger Things* and blockbuster books like *Firestarter*, always had those with special powers being studied and dissected in the name of science and national security.

"My sources inside the various agencies haven't heard anything, but it's a possibility. Think you can handle it?"

"No worries. I'll figure it out."

A cocky claim that proved harder to achieve than expected. For one, Ottawa sprawled over quite a distance. Two, the local pack refused to meet with her, citing they didn't like to deal with outsiders. At least the Ottawa Coven agreed to talk with her. Not exactly surprising since they were the ones to notify Colony Coven—the main coven that ruled over the rest in North America—of the disappearances of their members.

Clarabelle met them in a Starbucks of all places, the witches each sipping a different foamy brew. Five women in total, ranging in age with one thing in common; a weak affinity for magic. They eyed Clarabelle with curiosity.

The oldest of them greeted her first. "Hi, I'm Jewel, and these are my sisters, Kandy, Gertrude, Nelly, and Fiona."

Seeing as how Jewel hadn't done anything to protect their conversation, Clarabelle flicked her hands quickly to settle a dome of privacy over them, which widened some eyes. "Hello, I'm Clarabelle Montgomery, Colony Coven attaché. Sorry to meet you under such circumstances."

"Thanks for coming. We didn't know what else to do," Jewel apologized.

"You did the right thing. Can anyone tell me anything about the missing witches?" Clarabelle asked.

The youngest of the group, Kandy, with enough piercings to make Clarabelle leery of her spell-casting, given metal distorted, had a theory. "Maybe Felicia and Molly ran off together because they're in love."

"With none of their things?" scoffed Fiona, whose fiery red hair didn't come naturally.

Kandy didn't seem daunted by her retort. "Minimalist living is a growing trend."

Before Fiona could mock the girl, Gertrude, with her gray hair pinned in a chignon, snorted. "Don't be an idiot and stop sniffing so much toad juice. They disappeared a month apart, and you know damned well Felicia was engaged to that lawyer in the Glebe."

"Only the two gone?" Clarabelle clarified.

"We thought there was a third, but Gloria, unlike the others, cleared out her apartment. Most likely she joined another group. Not a big loss. She lacked a willingness to follow the rules," explained Jewel.

"Did they mention anything suspicious? Maybe someone following them? Emails? Texts?"

The women shook their heads.

The shyest member, Nelly, from behind her long bangs, whispered, "Do you think we're in danger?"

Much as she wanted to reassure, Clarabelle remained honest. "Until we know what's going on, you might want to take precautions. Don't go anywhere by yourself. Report anything that seems odd. Put protection spells on your doors and windows. Check-in with each other often."

Not the news they wanted to hear. The meeting broke up not long after, and Clarabelle found herself musing on what she'd learned. Not much other than it felt like foul play. Women, even witches, didn't disappear without packing at least a bag. As she walked back to her hotel, while deep in thought, she still paid attention to her surroundings and immediately felt it when someone started to stare.

Rather than turn around to peek, she cast a spell of surveillance on the clip holding her hair back. It recorded what it saw and she watched it once she returned to her hotel, which turned out to not be as interesting as expected. The replay showed some big blond dude staring after her before heading into a bar.

Just in case, she stored his image. After all, if witches were being targeted then she could be next.

2

With his head pounding painfully, Dracin woke inside a cage.

A fucking cage!

He had no one to blame but himself. Dracin had come into the city to pick up a part for his truck. He'd been heading back to said vehicle when his attention got distracted by an interesting scent. The intriguing odor had him staring at a woman, trim and petite, her hair drawn back with a barrette. She strode with brisk confidence, not once turning to look, despite his rude interest.

Run after her, his inner beast demanded, but instead of stalking a stranger, he chose to distract himself by getting a drink. Dracin didn't have that many, just a few shots of burning whiskey that should have barely given him a buzz, yet he'd staggered out of that bar into the night, wavering on his feet, seeing double.

Had someone roofied him? Possible, given he'd been elbow to elbow with strangers. And he had turned from his drink at one point to look over at the commotion caused by two guys arguing loudly. Had something been slipped in at that point?

Didn't matter. He'd planned to sleep it off in his truck. A plan that failed, seeing as how some assholes jumped him as he was passing out in an alley on his way to the parking lot.

Four of them. It should have been a cakewalk to beat their asses, only Dracin's reflexes were slow. His vision blurry. He'd swiped and missed. Bad luck seeing as one of his assailants got him in the face with a water balloon that exploded. Dracin roared in rage, ready to beat some ass, only his beast couldn't emerge.

The balloon held some kind of sleeping drug. The bastards came prepared.

Dracin passed out, and the result? He woke up in a fucking cage.

Not for long.

A grab of the bars sent him reeling and hissing; the skin on his fingers blistering right away. The electricity coursing through the enclosure holding him made it clear someone didn't want him to break out.

Joke was on them. Dracin just had to shift, and he'd be out of here. He might be fragile in this, his human form, but his beast? A lot tougher.

Wake up. He tried rousing his inner animal, to no avail. Whatever they'd drugged him with lingered in his system.

Goddammit!

Once he escaped, someone would pay. *I am going to eat whoever is responsible.*

If he escaped...

He had no choice. He'd not lived this long to die so ignobly.

Maybe he could shock his beast out of its sleep. He threw himself at the bars and held on tight, the current jolting his body hard enough he blacked out. He regained consciousness to find himself drooling on the floor. Of course at his most humiliated moment would be when his captor showed up to be annoying.

"Rise and shine, buttercup. Let's get a closer look at what my lackeys dragged in." The fellow who spoke wore a suit and had slicked-back hair. Young, but with the attitude of someone much older.

Finally, someone to direct his anger at. Dracin rose, seething at the sight of the man before him. Not just a man. A sniff had him frowning. "What are you?" Because he'd never smelled anything like the guy before.

"I'm insulted you don't know." The man flashed some fangs. "Does this help?

A fucking vampire? "Is that supposed to impress me? Mine are bigger, and if you don't want your first and last sight of them to be when I bite you in half, then you'll release me at once, bloodsucker."

"Is that any way to talk to the guy in charge of your fresh meat?"

"Don't make me tell you again," he stated, not that

he planned to let the fucker off easy. Hell no. He'd make him regret ever daring to think he could cage Dracin.

"Whine all you like. I'm not letting you go. I've got plans for you."

"Fuck your plans."

The vampire shook his head. "Terrible manners. But those can be beaten into you. And speaking of manners, where are mine? I'm Theodore, and you are?"

"Going to make you regret your life choices."

"So fiery. What fun I'll have breaking you, Dracin Smith. Interesting first name, by the way. Unique. Yet, oddly, there is little known about you. A good thing we have your wallet, or we might have never even gotten that much."

"What do you want?"

"What does anyone want in this world? Money. Lots of it."

"Well, you kidnapped the wrong guy then."

The vamp chuckled. "Oh, you're hilarious. Who knew dragons could be so entertaining?"

The fucker knew Dracin's shifter side. That didn't bode well. People often assumed the stories of dragons having invaluable hoards were true. Dracin wished. His single mom had done her best to raise him, but they'd gone without quite often. Even now, he didn't have much. He worked and made only enough to pay his bills.

"Don't know what you're talking about," Dracin lied.

"Don't be shy. I have to admit to being delighted my lackeys found you. When they told me they found a strange-smelling shifter, I thought you just needed a bath. But the moment I got a whiff, I knew. You're not the first one I've ever met. Alas, your predecessor escaped. My fault. I wasn't as prepared the last time. I've improved my methods since." Spoken with a smile that would have done a shark proud.

"You're wasting your time. I'm not rich."

"Oh. I'm aware you're not. Living in a shack outside of the city. Driving a beat-up truck. You really make dragons look bad."

"Listen. you pompous asshole—"

"No, you listen," Theodore hissed, drawing close. "Here is what's going to happen. You're going to get cleaned up because I've got buyers coming. People interested in owning their very own dragon. AKA you."

"You would enslave me?" He couldn't help the shocked reply.

"That depends on your new owner," Theodore declared with a shrug. "Once they buy you, it's up to them what they do. Chain you up, set you free, fuck you, hunt you, that's really up to them to decide once they pay."

His beast chose that moment to drowsily awake and growl, a low, inhuman sound.

The vamp grinned. "Seems like the drugs are

wearing off. Good. The buyers will want to see what they're bidding on."

"I'm going to eat you." He would, even though he could tell by the smell that vampire meat would taste bad.

"So bloodthirsty. I like it. I totally understand. I want to eat everyone who annoys me too. A good thing I don't, or I'd have no one left to work for me." Theodore offered a toothy grin.

Dracin had heard enough. With his beast awake, time to blow this joint. "Last chance to run, asshole." He called on his dragon. Only nothing happened.

"Uh-oh, is someone having a problem shifting? This is probably a good time to mention the device we implanted. It's the newest technology in controlling pets. With the press of a button inside this handy app, I can... You know what, how about I show you?" The vamp held out his phone and tapped the screen.

Instant agony hit and dropped Dracin to his knees. Holy fucking pain.

"Oops. Does that hurt? Good. That's the punishment setting. It has different levels, and even better, the app can be programmed to accept voice commands from your owner so as to prevent accidents. We implemented it after the incident where a pet knocked the phone out of its owner's hands and before he could recover it, well... Let's just say he didn't survive. I'm proud to reveal we've improved on it since then." Theodore sounded so pleased.

Dracin's stomach plummeted. "You fucker..."

"Is that an invitation? Alas, I have to refuse. I learned the last time I had a dragon in my grips that your blood is quite foul. Really disgusting." Theodore made a moue. "Pity. I'll bet you'd have made an excellent blood slave. Now if you'll excuse me, I've much to do to get ready for the auction. Already there is much interest, and I am expecting a rather large crowd. I can't wait to see the bidding. Just so you know, potential buyers will be popping by for a peek. Try being nice to the ones that appeal. Or stay feisty. Up to you. I know a few that prefer a savage to make things interesting whether it be for fighting or sex."

Dracin growled, but the unimpressed vamp waggled his fingers and left.

Fucking dick. When he got out…

More like if.

Dracin took stock of the situation. Outside his cage he noticed two more, smaller and empty. Only his had a thick wire running across the floor. A glance overhead showed his enclosure stood ten feet tall, big enough for him to shift if that fucker hadn't done something to prevent it.

The damp concrete floor hinted of mildew but, more annoying, the pungent aroma and noticeable lumps of rat scat. It reminded him of the shitholes he grew up in, the things he'd done to survive. He'd promised himself he'd never eat rat again. He really hoped he didn't have to break that promise.

The basement had no windows but did have a few pillars and the remnants of faint lines on the floor. An abandoned parking garage, making it unlikely anyone would hear or find him. A human-sized door marked the exit on one side, and on the other, a ramp that angled upward and around a corner finished off the space. Nothing useful.

Next, he did a check of his belongings and body. He wore his clothes but lacked his phone and wallet. Though he appeared uninjured, the implant concerned him. He ran his hands over his flesh, seeing if he could find the entrance wound, but there was none. His shifter healing patched him up too damned fast.

He had to find the device being used to control him. Only how? He palpated his flesh to no avail.

Hungry. His dragon didn't seem to care they were in a cage with no food. It eyed the rat that boldly crept into view.

No, Dracin replied.

Hungry. A plaintive demand.

"I said fucking no," Dracin snapped, which led to his big bad beast sulking, which didn't help his pounding head.

An urge to piss left him eyeing the bucket left for him and gave him an idea. While he really wanted to whizz on the bars, he remembered a Darwin award given to a dude who'd gotten drunk, climbed some kind of electrical pole, and let loose on the wire. He died because electricity and urine didn't play well together.

He could still use that knowledge, but, being a

smart guy, Dracin filled the bucket instead. The pungent smell made him grimace. This had better work. Being careful to hold only the plastic parts of his bucket, he poured his piss on the bars then stood back while it sizzled and popped. The lights flickered. He knew his plan worked when the humming stopped.

Next problem, the bars.

He grabbed hold and pulled. They didn't budge. He'd kind of expected that.

"All right, big guy, your turn to try."

The sulking dragon within instantly perked up. Surely the device couldn't control the shift as the vampire boasted. Most likely the drugs still affected him, but if he tried hard enough, his beast could break through. It had to.

Dracin closed his eyes as his beast began to surge and—

He woke on the floor, head pounding worse than before, not improved by his whimpering dragon.

It was true. The fucking implant and not lingering drugs impeded his ability to shift.

"Corpse fucker! Argh!" Dracin yelled, unable to quell his frustration.

If he couldn't escape, he was well and truly screwed. No one would come to the rescue. Dracin took living a solitary life quite seriously. Hardly any friends. No family since Mom died ages ago. Just him. And now that he found himself truly alone, he kind of regretted that choice. Then again, friendships weren't exactly easy to make for a guy like him. The werewolves had their packs and tended to not socialize outside them. Other non-humans, while rare, tended to steer clear of him. He blamed Hollywood for making them think dragons ate everyone who got close—as if they could compare to a tender hunk of beef. Of course, when it came to humans, he'd yet to meet one he didn't want to eat after a while. Hmm, maybe Hollywood wasn't entirely far off.

Forget a girlfriend. Dracin fucked only when he really got tired of his hand. It wasn't that he didn't like women, just that, after sex, he tended to eye them and think, *not the one*. As if there was someone for an ornery bastard like him.

The melancholy roused his annoyance, and Dracin yanked once more on the bars, only to bellow as they sizzled his flesh again. They'd reset the breaker while he was passed out.

"You fucking bastard. I am going to hunt your scrawny ass. I will pluck out your eyes like grapes. Remove your head and shove it up your ass. Come here and face me, you coward." At least give him a chance to fight.

No one replied to his challenge.

For the first time since he'd escaped the poverty that plagued his childhood, Dracin felt despair. The digging fingers of dread gripped him tight, urging him to give up hope.

But he refused to yield.

He'd not given up when lying on the ground, cold and hungry.

He'd not given up when, as a small and ill-dressed boy, he gotten beaten up.

He'd not given up when his mother, the only person he'd ever loved, died in a hit-and-run.

No. He'd clawed his way out of poverty. He'd gotten his revenge on those who hurt him. Found the fucker who murdered his mom and had him arrested.

He'd find a way out of this clusterfuck too.

In the meantime, he had to survive. But forget playing nice.

When Theodore returned later that day, bringing the first of the clients, Dracin ignored them. Chose pain over doing tricks.

No, he would not shift.

No, he wouldn't play their game.

And so he suffered.

And waited.

Waited for his chance to escape.

3

THE BREAK IN THE CASE OF THE MISSING WITCHES happened by accident.

In the days since her arrival, Clarabelle had been doing her best to investigate with little to go on. The pack refused to talk despite repeated requests. The only reason she knew about the missing werewolves at all was because of a whistleblower, who'd never contacted the coven again.

Jewel had arranged for her to check out the apartments of the missing women to no avail. Clarabelle even visited the vacant condo of a warlock—the male version of a witch, and much rarer—whose lover claimed he'd just upped and disappeared on the eve of their trip to Cuba. Supposedly, Francois had been on his way home, his last text sent before he boarded the subway. By all indications, he never got off. Given he was the most recent of the missing persons, Clarabelle tried scrying for his location, only to have to tell a grieving lover that the lack of response from the spell most likely meant he was dead.

That same scrying spell had failed as well with the witches. One showed a useless image of a tree not local to the area, and the other also indicated death.

Very concerning, and annoying. Clarabelle didn't like being stymied. On her way back from a visit to a local restaurant where she'd hoped to find a bartender named Olive who used to date the missing half-elf, she found herself sighing and wondering if it was time to speak to Marjorie about maybe convening a circle of thirteen to contact the Lord Hades. The god of death and Hell might be able to shed some light on their case —the problem being the cost he'd demand. Finding thirteen powerful witches willing to participate and risk their lives to help others wouldn't be easy.

At not quite midnight and almost in sight of her hotel, Clarabelle found herself surprised when a vampire stepped out of the alley. To a human, the man would have seemed normal, if pale. To a witch, the absence of life and magic provided a dead giveaway—pun intended.

"Well, well, if it isn't my lucky night. Hello, little witch." The vampire showed off baby fangs that would have made a cobra laugh.

It would take a lot more than that to impress Clarabelle, but rather than put him in his place, she decided to play along and pretend she couldn't turn him into a pile of ash.

"Evening. I didn't realize there was a clan in

Ottawa." The vampires tended to be sorted by makers, with the one doing the making heading the clan. Given most of the turned went mad quickly, the clans never tended to be too large, with the unfit quickly exterminated. No clan wanted a repeat of the bloodbath on Roanoke Island. People assumed a natural disaster led to the town fleeing. Not really. The clans cleaned up after their own and, in this case, went scorched earth to prove a point. No letting the weak roam.

"My Lord tends to keep a low profile." He eyed her up and down. "You must be new to the coven."

"Just here visiting," she trilled. "Always fun to trade recipes." She intentionally made herself seem flighty.

It worked. He licked his lips. "If you're looking for some action, I know a place."

"What kind of action?" She pretended as if she didn't know of the treaty between witches and vampires, the one that banned his kind from snacking on hers, brokered at the behest of the vampires who found themselves in a bad spot when they ate the wrong witch centuries ago. At times, Clarabelle wondered why her ancestors bothered letting the bloodsuckers live.

"The kind of action your Lord Hades approves of."

She highly doubted it given Satan didn't like vampires since, as the undead, they'd never serve him in Hell. "Is it far?"

"Nope." He popped the p, and his smile meant to look reassuring came off as too eager.

Could he be involved in the missing witches? A

vampire could recognize not only a witch but other non-humans by scent alone. They had a fine-tuned sense when it came to blood. Of course, that would mean they were breaking treaty. Could it be this clan thought themselves above the laws? Only one way to find out.

"Sounds like more fun than I had planned. Lead the way," she stated, still with a fake smile plastered on.

No surprise, the vampire took her through some sketchy alleys, past avarice-filled gazes, not that anyone dared accost, given who guided her.

She made small talk. "What's your name? I'm Lara." She changed her name in case he'd heard of her.

"Clive."

"Have you been part of the clan for long?"

"A few months, but I'm already high up in the hierarchy." He puffed out his chest.

She didn't point out that rank and position came with age. Vampires truly needed time to develop their powers. The oldest ones posed the most danger given the ability to mesmerize increased as they aged. A young fellow, like Clive, basically had teeth and a bit of strength, not much more.

"Seems like Ottawa is quite the place for witches and others what with having its own pack, a coven, even some elves. And now, vampires," she gushed.

"That's just the tip of it," Clive confided. "The river and sewers have some kelpies, and there even used to be a mermaid."

"Used to?"

"She's gone now." No elaboration, but a hint Clarabelle might be on the right track.

They entered a sketchy part of town with hardly any lights and a few buildings sporting boarded windows. Seeing her wary glance, Clive murmured, "Revitalization area. Our leader bought the whole block. Gonna make it into a proper compound with tunnels linking the buildings underground."

"Grandiose vision considering a city this size means the clan would have been approved for, what? A dozen?" Part of the treaty established a maximum number of vamps dependent on the city size. One vamp per hundred thousand. Too late she realized she let on more than she should know about vampires.

Clive snickered. "Yeah, as if our leader cares what the council says he can do."

A reply that didn't reassure. Had they broken covenant? If yes, she could be headed towards trouble. Against one vamp, she could easily handle herself. But more than a handful? She'd better hope the Dark Lord listened to her prayers.

"How much farther?" she murmured.

"Right down there." The vamp pointed to a sloping ramp under one of the boarded buildings leading into a parking garage.

She halted. "I thought you said we were checking out the local action. I don't hear music."

"Soundproof walls," lied Clive.

She knew he lied because she heard a muffled roar beyond the supposed soundproofing. Moments later, people came scurrying out the door alongside the closed roll-down one for the garage. First a man dressed in a suit and a woman wearing heels and a faux fur coat. They were accompanied by a vampire, female this time, who barely cast Clive and Clarabelle a glance as she murmured to the couple, "Of course he'll come with the usual controls."

Words to make Clarabelle wonder, along with what sent them fleeing.

Clive used their appearance to say, "See. Told you all the action was down there."

"Then let's check it out." She saw it as a good sign the humans left without injury. Now, it remained to be seen if the same could be said of Clive. She didn't like him and hoped he gave her a reason to end his undead existence. The treaty had several conditions whereupon she could kill him without penalty.

The keypad by the door appeared new in comparison to everything else. Clive punched in six digits that she memorized. The door clicked and gave them entry into a place that immediately gave her goosebumps. It wasn't the smell of piss, blood, and animal that did it, but the cool tingle that warned this place had seen more than its fair share of death and violence.

She kept her hands ready to cast as she followed behind Clive, the ramp steep and the parking lot ahead empty until she turned the corner and got to see the full basement. Despite the faded lines on the floor, it held no cars, just a few cages.

"What is this? Where's the party?" Her tone remained light.

"You're looking at it, witch." Clive remained blithely smirking.

She'd have permanently wiped it from his face if she didn't have questions. "Looks kind of dull if you ask me." As she spoke, she noticed movement in the largest cage. A man stood, a big man, familiar too. It took a second to recall she'd seen him in that spying spell she'd placed on her barrette. He'd been the guy staring at her a few days ago.

And now he was trapped in a cage.

"Don't you worry, little witch. Things are about to get freaky." The vamp grinned. "But being a nice guy, I'll give you a choice. Cage on the left or the right?"

"Not happening." She maintained her reasonable tone. "You do realize this is against the treaty between our kind."

"Fuck the treaty."

"Does your leader know you're messing with witches?"

"Who do you think gave us the order to bring them in? While your kind don't bring the highest price, every dollar counts." He grinned widely, cocky and sure he held the upper hand.

Meanwhile, he appeared to have confessed. "You're the one behind the disappearances of the cryptids," she stated flatly.

"Not just me. It's a joint effort," he boasted.

"The capture and sale of witches is prohibited."

"Like I said before, fuck the treaty."

She arched a brow. "Big words. You do know that those who contravene the articles of it are subjected to culling."

"Only if someone finds out. Which they won't. We've been doing this for a while," he boasted, sealing his fate.

"Kind of cocky of you to be admitting your crimes."

"Who you going to tell?" he scoffed.

"Oh, Clive. You really have no idea who you're messing with, do you?" She shook her head.

"No, you're the one who's in trouble." He still didn't get it.

The steps approaching from behind might have been quiet enough to sneak up on a human but not a witch who'd wrapped herself in a defense spell from the moment she'd met the vampire. She let their new third party continue to stalk her as she focused on the idiot in front of her.

Clive stared, his eyes turning into black pits as he whispered, "Get in the cage."

His attempt to mesmerize her failed to have any effect.

"I don't think so," Clarabelle's pert reply.

He frowned and concentrated more intently. "Get in the cage, now!"

"I'd tell you to bite me, but you'd think I was flirting," Clarabelle stated calmly. "And to whoever thinks they can sneak up on me, be warned. Any attempts at harm will be hazardous to your health."

"I'm going to enjoy breaking you," Clive snarled. "Get her, Harriet."

"Don't say I didn't warn you," Clarabelle sweetly replied. As the female behind her reached to grab, Clarabelle murmured a single word that strengthened her magical shield. The effect? The hand that tried to touch ignited.

Screaming ensued.

Clarabelle didn't bother turning around.

"The bitch lit me on fire," screeched the female as she ran past Clarabelle, whole arm ablaze and the flames still climbing.

Clive narrowed his gaze. "You think you're so clever. Let's see how you fare against someone stronger."

"Are you stronger? Let's find out, shall we?" She stared at him, her turn now to push a mental order. "Hands on your head."

Compulsion spells were something all witches learned early on as part of their defense training. Unlike shapeshifters—who were immune to magic—a weak vampire, still close to its human roots, would be affected by them.

Clive cupped his crown and glared at her. "You won't get away with this."

"Funny, I was about to say the same. Come, let's go see who you've got in the big cage. Then, you can tell me all about your operation."

A stiff-legged Clive marched while the imprisoned man eyed them, silent, yet no doubt listening to every word.

"Start talking," she ordered Clive. "Who's your leader? What's he been doing?"

"Theodore Beaumont rules in Ottawa. He originally belonged to the Toronto clan but was granted permission to start his own in Ottawa a few decades ago." So still relatively new.

"Why is he selling witches and others?" she asked.

"Money. He got tired of living like a pauper. He tried asking the council for funds but was told clans build wealth over time."

True, mostly because being long-lived meant their investments had time to mature. It also helped they could mesmerize some of their sheep into donating to their coffers. "So he decided to kidnap nonhumans and sell them?"

"There's a market for them. People will pay big money for the rare and exotic."

"To do what with them?" she asked, even as her stomach churned. She doubted she'd like the answer.

"Whatever the buyer wants. Most like owning them as a trophy. The mermaid's in some indoor pool in Switzerland. An elf ended up as a house servant for some rich guy in Banff."

They stopped by the big cage and the quietly glowering guy. Not a warlock. He didn't have the right kind of aura. She glanced at the vampire and chided him. "Selling people is wrong, Clive."

"Only if caught."

She couldn't stand to listen to him anymore. "The council will be informed of your clan's crimes."

"As if you'll make it out of here a—"

She interrupted. "I've heard quite enough from you. I told you that you messed with the wrong witch." Her hand lifted, and with a simple command—*Push*—magic slammed into Clive and tossed him against the bars of the cage.

Barely a shove, and yet he screamed and screamed, the singe of burning flesh caused by the electrified bars.

A rather toasty Clive fell to the floor, his mouth open and shutting as if gasping for air, which was funny since vampires didn't need to breathe unless they wanted to talk.

She knelt and cocked her head. "By the power invested in me by the Dracula Treaty and the Colony Coven, I hereby find you guilty of the incarceration and sale of witches and other nonhumans. The penalty is death." She flicked her fingers, and Clive ignited, so fast and fierce he didn't have time to scream.

As she rose to her feet, a gruff voice warned, "Behind you."

She didn't bother whirling, just tossed more magic over her shoulder as the female she'd already partially roasted came rushing back—and died.

"Any more of them around?" she asked the man in the cage.

"Not currently, but I've counted seven different vamps since my capture. They come and go once it gets dark."

She eyed him, his height well over six feet, broad of

shoulder, jaw scruffy and blond like the hair crowning his head. A veritable modern-day Viking. "How long since they nabbed you?"

"A few days, I think. Hard to tell given how many times they knocked me out."

"You're nonhuman I assume."

"Shifter."

Meaning her magic wouldn't work on him, but then again, why would he pose a danger to the person trying to rescue him? "The bars are electrified." Stated more than asked.

"Yes."

"Give me a moment while I disable it." While Clive might have shorted them out when he landed on them, she'd rather not jolt herself finding out.

She tracked the wire from the cage to a wall outlet torn open so that the wiring could be spliced. She wrapped her hand in a magical glove before pulling the pigtails apart. As she returned to the enclosure, she noticed the man watching her.

"I'm Clarabelle, by the way," she stated.

"Dracin." A pause then, "You're a witch?"

"What gave it away?" she teased with an arched brow. "So speaking of magic, I'm going to use some to open your cage. Once I do, I'd advise you to either get out of town or lie really low because I doubt the vampires will be happy with what's transpired here."

"I wasn't planning on sticking around."

"Good. Stand by while I handle the lock."

He took a step away, and she eyed the mechanism

before shrugging. She'd never been good at lock-picking magic. She blasted it instead.

The door swung open, and he immediately stepped out, but he didn't run. "Thank you."

"You're welcome. I don't suppose you saw anyone else in the cages?"

He shook his head. "Whoever was in them was long gone before my arrival."

"Pity." She pursed her lips. "How did they capture you?"

"Drugged my drink, unlike you. Do you always accompany vampires to deserted basements?"

"Only when my Friday nights are boring," she quipped.

He frowned at her. "You could have been captured."

"But wasn't."

A glower went well with his grumbled, "Unlike me. Can't believe I had to be saved."

He took a few long strides before looking over his shoulder at her. "Aren't you coming?"

"I need to investigate further. You're not the only person they captured."

"You're a detective witch?" His brows rose impressively high.

"Of sorts. I was tasked by the coven to look into some recent disappearances, which might number more than we imagine given you never made it into my file." Her lips pursed.

"How many have been taken?"

"That we know of? A pair of wolves, two witches, a warlock, and a half-elf. Clive also alluded to a mermaid."

"That's just the tip of the iceberg. I'm picking up more than two dozen scents alone in here," Dracin confirmed.

"How brazen. I have to say, of all the things I expected to find, a vampire clan participating in nonhuman trafficking never made the list."

"What did you expect?" he asked.

"Serial killer. Although government kidnapping was a close second."

He blinked. What beautiful long lashes he had. She wondered what kind of shifter he was. Wolf? Bear? With that blond hair, maybe a rare lion?

"You mean to say you thought you might be dealing with a serial killer and still blithely followed Clive into this basement?"

"How else was I supposed to confirm he was involved?" She rolled her eyes. "Now if you'll excuse me, I need to see if there's any clues as to the whereabouts of the others before I burn this place down."

"Why burn it?"

She might have been channeling her Dark Lord a bit when she offered a low, "To let this Theodore and his clan know I'm coming for them."

4

Saved by a witch. Not something Dracin would have guessed would happen in a million years. For one, given his rather constrained upbringing, he never even knew they existed—or that a witch would be so cute.

And deadly.

She'd appeared innocuous when she first arrived. Another hapless victim he couldn't help. In silence from behind his bars, he'd watched her giving the vampire attitude. Expected her to get hurt when that female bloodsucker had been sneaking up behind her, only the witch wiggled her fingers and *blam*. She'd set the threat on fire.

Impressive, but even more surprising? His dragon's reaction.

Mine. A no-argument, no-doubt statement from his beast that this petite and feisty woman was meant to be his mate.

His.

Fucking.

Mate.

Which might not have been so bad but for the fact the first time they met face to face she had to come to his rescue because his weak ass couldn't get out of a cage. Way to *not* impress. As if he cared what she thought. Once he left the garage, they'd never see each other again.

Want.

No, his reply to his beast. Despite what his dragon thought, he didn't want a mate.

Apparently, she didn't either, given she ignored his ass and stalked across to the other cages. Crouching down to peek. Wiggling her fingers and making the concrete floor glow. She made not a sound as she worked. Neither did he as he watched, which might have explained her surprise when she turned and saw him. "How come you're still here?"

"Just making sure the vamps don't return and put you in one of those things." He indicated the cage.

Her nose wrinkled. "As if it could hold me."

"I thought the same."

"Fear not. While you might not be able to channel electricity, I can. I can also bend those bars. So, you see, nothing to worry about."

The arrogance stunned. Mostly because he'd been so sure he could easily surmount his imprisonment as well. For a fleeting second, he debated not mentioning Theodore's nasty implant that prevent him from acting. But what if Theodore returned and she counted on Dracin as backup and that fucker took him out with the press of a button. "The vamps put something inside me."

She paused her stalking toward the far wall to eye him. "They molested you?" She completely misunderstood.

"No!" he huffed, partially horrified. "They surgically inserted some kind of device. I don't know exactly what, but it's small enough I can't feel it. It is powerful, though. With the press of a button, they can render me unconscious. They can also constrain my beast." A beast she'd yet to ask about. She probably thought him some mangy dog.

Ack. The very idea had his dragon just about having a conniption.

A whistle emerged from her perfect full lips. "Well, that's unexpected. Where did they insert it?"

His shoulders rolled. "No idea. By the time I knew what they'd done, the injection site had healed over."

"Hmm. Shouldn't be too hard to find given it's a foreign object. Stand still while I look."

Being told to not move made him want to fidget, especially since she stood close.

Bite her.

We are not biting.

But she's ours.

No, she's not.

His dragon pouted.

He didn't entirely blame the beast. The witch oozed

sexy. She also probably had her picture under the definition of feisty. But he'd been controlling himself for a long time now. Surely he could handle a few minutes of close proximity.

Luckily, she didn't waste time.

Her eyes went out of focus, and he could see a soft golden glow around her. She paced around him before she murmured, "I think I found it. Stem of your skull, embedded in the brain matter."

The word embedded almost made him wince. He should count himself lucky he didn't wake a vegetable. "Can you remove it?"

"Maybe, but not here."

"Where then?"

She pursed her lips. "My hotel room won't be adequate. The extraction will require boiling water to sterilize among other things. I'll talk to the coven about borrowing a kitchen."

"I have a kitchen," he blurted out.

"What about a sharp knife?"

His lips quirked. "I hunt and process meat, so yeah."

"It will be painful. Do you have analgesics? Something to numb the pain?"

"Would whiskey count?"

Her lips quirked. "So long as you keep a glass for me when I'm done."

"Deal."

"Very well. Once I'm finished here, we will proceed to your place for the removal."

"There ain't anything else to see here." He indicated the barren parking garage.

She glanced upward. "Are the floors above deserted?"

"No idea. But I didn't hear anything, and the vamps only ever came in through the main entrance." He indicated the ramp.

"Given the concrete ceiling, you might not have noticed. Let's go take a peek."

While he wanted nothing more than to leave this fucking place, he found himself shadowing her brisk steps, enjoying a little too much the wiggle of her ass in her slim-fitting slacks. Her fleece-lined jacket ended just an inch below her waist. Classy yet practical attire. He wore a simple tracksuit, given to him after they hosed him off in between visits by prospective buyers. Nothing like shivering with cold in soggy jeans to agree to swap garments. He might be ornery, but he preferred to not add stupid to that list. Just like he'd not rejected the food and water they brought. Couldn't escape if he was weak from hunger and dehydration.

They had to use the stairwell since the elevator had an out-of-order sign. She nimbly climbed the steps, and he resisted an urge to tell her to slow down and let him go first. It was as if she wanted to rush headlong into danger. The only reason he didn't pull an alpha male and insist? The lack of any recent scents. He could have told her no one had been by in quite some time, but he had a feeling she'd still insist on taking a look.

As expected, the first floor showed no signs of habitation. Just a bunch of empty offices, a few still with cheap desks and chairs.

Same on the second level. "There's nothing here," he stated once they hit the third floor without seeing anything of worth.

Hands planted on her hips as she pursed her lips. "Agreed, which means they're keeping the paperwork on the sales elsewhere."

"Assuming they're tracking it. After all, what they're doing is illegal," he pointed out.

"The vampires are meticulous when it comes to business. They'll have records for a few reasons. One, to document who bought what and how much they paid. Two, it provides them with a means to blackmail. And three, because they're cocky assholes who think they're above the laws."

The expletive shocked and roused admiration. "You're not frightened by this at all."

"No. And neither are you. You're angry," she stated.

"Ya think?" his sarcastic reply. "The fuckers drugged me by slipping something in my whiskey at the bar. Which is a sacrilege on its own. Then they jumped me on my way to my truck and gave me another dose. I woke up in the cage. Unable to shift. The bars electrified." He grimaced. "A fucking zoo animal they kept showing off to those with money."

"You saw some of their clients?"

"Yeah."

"Any names? Descriptions?"

"You plan on hunting them down?"

She turned a dark gaze on him. "The buyers are just as guilty as the sellers. Could be we'll find some of the others who were taken. We also need to ensure they don't do it again or reveal what they know."

"Going to kill them?"

"They'll be handled according to coven law."

"Which says what in this kind of case?"

Her lips curved. "No mercy for those who trespass against us."

She headed for the stairs, him trailing after her, impressed by her determination and heroic nature. For a guy who did his own thing and kept to himself, that kind of selfless behaviour confused and intrigued.

Hero. His dragon had a name for it.

She opened the door to the stairwell and entered without pause. He just managed to slap his hand on the portal before it shut and he instantly stiffened.

Not alone. He sensed more than smelled someone below. He leaped to land lightly in front of her on the first turn, finger to his lips.

Rather than speak, she nodded and let him take the lead. Knowing danger waited had him flexing with adrenaline. Dracin dearly wanted to hit something. He resisted the urge to crack his knuckles lest he warn the vamps below they were coming. They probably already knew, given their finely tuned hearing and sense of smell.

He could only hope Theodore with his dreaded app wasn't among them because he'd hate to be reduced to a slobbering fool on the floor while Clarabelle fought by herself.

The vampires kept quiet, waiting to pounce. Rather than stroll into their midst, he vaulted over the railing, landing in a crouch to see three bloodsuckers.

Their eyes widened only a second before their fangs came out.

Let me eat them.

His beast totally wanted to emerge and chomp, but that wasn't feasible for two reasons, one, the confined space, and two, the block against shifting remained in effect. A good thing he'd become handy with his fists when his mom enrolled him in Muay Thai and wrestling after she got tired of excuses by the principal at school as to why her son was being bullied. It had helped him as a teen, when he'd sprouted and girls started eyeing him, leading to jealous guys thinking they could take their frustrations out on him—they learned not to really quick. As an adult, Dracin frequented dive bars, the kind where he could drink alone, the only problem being it attracted other loner types, who, after a few too many beers, started picking fights.

All this to say, he wasn't afraid to hit. And hit hard. Vamps weren't humans, though, and could take a walloping. They were also strong, fast, and liked to fucking bite.

"Keep those teeth to yourself, bloodsucker!" He'd better be immune to their bite. He had no interest in becoming one.

Just as he readied to end the fight, Clarabelle appeared. "Anyone in the mood for some sunshine?" the dulcet question before a bright light flooded the stairwell. The shrieks of the vampires went with their panic as they tried to escape the illumination. They dove through the nearest door to escape.

He glared at the witch. "I was handling it."

"You were playing with them, and I have better things to do."

"Yeah, well, brilliant plan. They're going to run off and tell their master I escaped."

"Are they?" she queried as she strode through the door after them. They'd reached the first floor, with the vacant offices, doors ajar, and so many places and shadows to hide. "Come out, come out wherever you are," she sang.

Crazy witch. Dracin stood back, not too far. and let her make a target of herself. The vampire couldn't resist and sprang from the ceiling where he'd been clinging like a bat.

Before Dracin could smack him aside, the witch caught him in a fist of air. "Hello there. And who might you be?"

Snarl.

"Not one of the smarter ones, are you? You won't do." With that, she ignited the vampire and dropped him. The screaming pyre ran off.

Harsh but Dracin liked her style.

She stalked farther down the hall and he followed a few paces behind. The next vampire blitzed from a doorway, all fangs and outstretched clawed fingers. She tsked. "You're barely more than an animal too. This clan really has strayed from the rules."

Another vampire ran off burning.

One, wait, make that two remained. Apparently, the stairwell trio had a fourth partner.

Clarabelle stood, arms crossed, waiting. Petite and unassuming. The idiots didn't pay attention to their burning brethren, that or their blood lust overruled common sense. They burst out into the open, rushing for her.

An upraised hand, all it took on her part, and they stopped as if they'd hit a wall.

She cocked her head. "Which one of you is going to live to tell your master his trafficking is over?"

"He'll kill you, witch. He'll suck you dry as he fucks you—"

A flick of her finger and the litany of threats ended, mostly because the vampire's head separated from the body.

Damn. She was strong. Could all witches do that?

She stared at the last vampire, who visibly gulped. "You will take my message," she stated, not asked.

His head bobbed.

"Good. Tell your leader, Theodore is his name I believe, that Clarabelle will be paying him a visit soon to discuss his transgressions. Understood?"

More frantic nodding.

"Begone before I change my mind. Oh, and you might want to apply to transfer to another clan. This one is done." Her last low threat. The vampire scurried off, and Dracin waited, leaning against a wall as she returned to his side.

"Was that really wise giving out your name like that?"

"I don't want him thinking it was someone from the local coven."

Wait, did she just imply there were more witches in the city?

"You do realize you just declared war on the vampires," he stated.

"I'm aware."

He felt a need to point out, "You're just one witch."

"I'm sure I can conscript some help if I feel it necessary, but if these pathetic minions are an example of what to expect, I don't think I have much to worry about. Now, if you're done chastising, I'd like to finish up here. All that spellcasting has left me famished."

"Has anyone ever told you that you're crazy?"

Her lips curved into a sweet smile that tightened his groin. "All the time. As a teen, when my powers kept manifesting and I didn't understand why, my parents had me institutionalized. They assumed I set the fires that kept cropping up with matches no one could find. They didn't believe I was doing it with magic." She waggled her fingers. "Luckily, a witch working in the hospital as a nurse recognized my problem as not being a mental one and got me into a coven-run school, where I was taught how to control myself."

Despite himself, he couldn't stem his curiosity. "How come your parents didn't teach you?"

She cast a glance at him. "I was an anomaly. Born of non-magic parents. Rare but not unheard of. I assume one of your parents was a shifter."

"My mom was," he admitted. "But she got cast out of her pack for hooking up with my dad, who wasn't."

"How archaic. I can't believe that, in today's world, anyone cares who one loves."

"Maybe people should care before they fuck up their kids," he muttered. His parents' forbidden relationship didn't stand the test of time. His dad left when he was born, and his mom never recovered. It didn't help that a wolf shifter didn't know what to do with a child who was also a dragon. Mom's response to that? Hide the fact he even existed. She seemed to think if people knew he'd be hunted. Given what he'd seen in movies? She most likely was right.

Clarabelle gave him a curious glance. "Not a believer in love?"

Yes. His dragon's reply.

"No," was what he said. He didn't believe the truemate bullshit his mother used to talk about. No matter how much this woman drew him, he would not succumb.

Nope.

Not happening.

Rather than let her magic blast a way out, he used his pent-up aggression to bust through the plywood covering a doorway on the main level. They spilled out onto the dark street.

Clarabelle gave him a light push. "Stand back while I send a message to the clan perpetrating the crime."

"Isn't that why we let one vamp go free?"

"I like to be thorough when it comes to making a point. Now, if you don't mind..." She lifted her hands.

He didn't move far. Why would he when the flames looked so pretty, licking at the plywood covering the windows? When she was satisfied, she glanced at him. "I'm hungry. This kitchen you mentioned, it has food?"

"Eggs and bacon okay?"

"Sounds delicious."

The pickup truck he'd parked at a meter had long since been towed, meaning they had to take an Uber, which she paid for. As if his emasculation wasn't already complete.

When she stood in front of the place he called home, he expected something disparaging about the small and very plain bungalow surrounded by forest.

Instead, she nodded and smiled. "Nice. Lots of privacy." Then cast him a side-eye before saying, "Let's see how well you cook."

He knew she meant in the kitchen, and yet he almost wanted to boast he could do much better in the bedroom.

Resist. He had to resist. Now if only she wouldn't make it so hard—like literally rock solid—when she made those happy noises while chewing her bacon—and not his cock.

5

Dracin wouldn't look at her directly. Most likely because he didn't like having her invading his space. At the same time, when he did actually glance over, she finally understood the word smolder. As in his eyes literally heated enough to make her warm. Not the version that required her to remove clothes to cool herself but the kind of warmth that nestled between the thighs and made her want to squirm.

It should be known she didn't usually have that type of reaction with men. For her, attraction tended to be about a person's mind and ability to converse, not because he filled out a pair of pants in a way that should be illegal.

Yet something about this man, this shifter, reminded her she was a woman, a desirable one at that. Not that anything would happen. For one, she had no interest in dating; two, she couldn't be distracted by sex given everything going on; and three, the coven had clear rules about witches and shifters. No hooking up with anyone that wasn't a witch or warlock. The mixing of species could have strange results, especially where children were involved.

According to what she'd been taught, even if a couple got past the problems with fertility, those mismatched pairings usually produced unviable, and even dangerous, offspring, Medusa being the most famous case of a lamia and a warlock getting together. In some cases, the pregnancy could be fatal to the gestating mother.

As recently as the last century, when a witch or warlock decided to flout the rules for love, sometimes the coven took pre-emptive action and sterilized the pair to ensure no unfortunate accidents. In these modern times, the ease of abortion and birth control had led to the coven relaxing their rules and allowing couples to handle their fertility on their own.

But that didn't mean they approved. A witch who married outside their kind would find themselves demoted, not something Clarabelle agreed with. A witch's ability had nothing to do with whom they loved. Tell that to the coven who insisted on following old rules—or to the ones who took more drastic action, and decided to make offenders disappear.

After Clarabelle finished the most delicious eggs and bacon with buttered toast, she felt revived enough to clap her hands and say, "So, where's the sharp knife?"

"Going to stab me?"

"Slice actually. We need to create an incision for the device to emerge. I'll also want clean clothes and a bowl of sterilized water, AKA boiled. The knife should also be put to a flame to burn off any bacteria."

He arched a brow. "I'm pretty sure we don't have to worry about infection. I'm a fast healer."

"Even fast healers can be taken down by blood contamination. We can't know if this device has a failsafe built in to prevent removal."

That led to him frowning. "Failsafe?"

"It could be that it explodes if tampered with."

"Pretty sure it's too small to be a bomb."

"Fine, then it might short circuit, frying your synapses," her shrugged reply.

His lips pressed into a line. "Is this your way of trying to talk me out of its removal?"

"It's me trying to warn you of the possible dangers. This is new technology. As such, we can't be sure what to expect. Knowing this, would you like to delay treatment so we can study it further? I can make arrangements for a deeper analysis. Although an MRI machine, the best option, won't be possible given this device most likely has metal components."

"Fuck waiting. I want it out." A firm reply.

"I figured as much. Let's get the supplies then."

He didn't speak as he gathered the items requested. She eyed the neat pile. "Any gauze?"

"Nah. No point given how I heal."

"What about a needle and thread?"

He snorted. "Do I look like I sew?"

"Better hope I can keep the hole small then."

"I'll be fine," he insisted.

With everything she needed at her fingertips, there was no point in wasting more time. "Sit down." She pointed to the chair she'd vacated—the only one in the kitchen, which meant he'd eaten while standing, leaning against the counter. Before listening to her directions, he cleared the dishes. He didn't pile them in the sink but rinsed them and put them right in the dishwasher. She had to admit being impressed by how clean he kept his place. While simple and worn, his home didn't have clutter or a mess. The floors appeared swept and regularly mopped. The countertops wiped down. Nothing soaking in his sink other than the pan he'd just used.

Finally, he plopped into the seat, rigid and stony-faced.

She snapped her fingers. "We forgot to grab the whiskey."

"Don't need it. I can handle the pain."

"Who says it's for you?" she joked. While not usually nervous about procedures, this one had her a little discomfited. Not the actual incision and extraction itself. She'd done this kind of thing before, usually with bullets and shards of embedded metal and wood. Nonhumans often found themselves victims of hunters and sometimes chose the coven for healing.

Her disquietude came from having to touch him. She found her heart pounding faster than usual. Her palms slightly sweaty. It made no sense.

He grabbed a bottle of whiskey from the cupboard, brand new she noticed as he cracked it and drank from it without a glass. Several swigs. Then he offered it to her.

She demurred. "I should probably wait until after."

"Just in case..." He rose and grabbed a glass, pouring a generous amount. "Now I don't have to worry about drinking it all on you."

"What happened to you can handle it?" she teased.

"I can, but my inner beast? Kind of freaked."

The way he spoke as if his animal had a mind of its own... Intriguing. She'd not had much to do with shifters since they usually kept to their packs. They never came to the coven for healing because magic didn't work on them.

Which suddenly had her blurting out, "Are you sure you don't want a doctor?"

"Getting cold feet?" He half turned in the chair.

"More like figuring I should mention magic doesn't work on shifters. While my plan is to try and use finely focused manipulation on the object alone, there is a chance your body rejects my efforts. Are you sure you still want to try?"

"Do it." A flat reply.

"What if I can't extract it?"

"Then we'll see. Now stop stalling and slice me open, Belle."

Belle. Usually she'd take offense at someone shortening her name. But from his lips...

Ugh. She needed to stop being distracted.

She positioned herself behind him, knife in hand, the blade still warm from the flame she'd run along its edge. She eyed his nape, the hair curling slightly but for one small shaved spot, the tendrils already growing in. A bull's-eye that meant she didn't have to draw a circle.

"Hope you don't mind getting blood on your shirt," her dumb quip as she geared herself to cut.

"Fucking rag is going in the trash." With that, he tore it off, leaving her staring at a lot of flesh.

So. Much. Flesh. His broad shoulders leading to muscled arms. Even his back looked like it worked out in sharp contrast to her soft frame. She wasn't unfit, but she definitely didn't exercise as much as she should.

"Well, you going to stare all night or cut?" His growled query had her jerking and almost dropping the knife.

She firmed up her grip, gave herself a mental shake, and took in a breath. "This will hurt. Don't move."

"Don't worry about me. I'm no stranger to cuts needing stitches."

The tip of the knife touched his skin, and before she could question her choices, she pushed in, the welling blood hiding the slice as she slitted him as deep as she dared.

She let the blood free flow and set down the knife before calling on her magic and directing it at the hole. A hole that was trying to close.

"Dammit, stop healing so fast," she grumbled. "I need to slice it again, wider this time."

"Stick your finger in it."

"What?"

"A finger or an object will slow it down," he offered with a shrug.

"I am not sticking my finger in your bloody hole."

"Whatever, then don't whine."

"Ugh, you are insufferable," she huffed as she sliced bigger this time in a letter X, and then, despite her squeamishness about it, she did poke a finger inside, grimacing at the squishy wetness then sucking in a breath as she touched the hard edge of the object.

"I can feel it."

"Then get it out."

Given it was fused somehow to his occipital bone, that would be tricky. Hence the magic. She closed her eyes and focussed, directing the tugging and pulling force on the object only, hoping to avoid the rejection by his shifter genes.

The object stubbornly refused to budge, and she grumbled, "Your body is fighting me."

"Keep trying. I'll try and help you."

She almost muttered "you can't help" when a strange sensation coated her magic, didn't just coat but aided it. Twined together, she guided, and the alien magic—the only word she had for it—mimicked what she tried to do, pulling at the device, loosening it from the bone, only to realize—

"It's got tendrils going through your skull to the brain."

"Then cut them," he growled. He made it sound simple.

She kept her eyes closed and manipulated her magic to be fine-tuned enough to shear, only the blood all over the filaments rejected her attempts. The alien magic learned enough to finish the task, snipping the strands until the object floated free. She removed her finger, but before she could grab the knife to pop it free, the tiny rectangular chip emerged in a flood of blood.

She snatched it and squinted at its gory-covered surface. Felt it pulse, faster and faster.

She had only a second to act. She wrapped it in a tight bubble of magic that stifled the mini explosion.

The moment she could, she dropped the shield, sensing exhaustion creeping. She wasn't done yet. She dabbed at his neck, the bloody flow already slowing, the hole smaller already. Before she could grumble about the lack of a needle, it began healing.

"How do you feel?" she asked, realizing he'd not spoken in a bit.

"Weird. I've never had someone use magic on me before."

She almost admitted she wasn't the one using it. Yet no denying whatever helped her was magic. Just not hers. But whose? Couldn't be his. Shifters were immune to magic.

Could it be the Lord Hades had chosen to help his witch?

"Where's that whiskey?" She grabbed the glass with a trembling hand, more tired than expected. She'd not realized how much she'd been pouring of herself into the extraction. Add in her expenditures earlier with the vampires and she was feeling rather lightheaded.

"Thanks," he said, standing, a large looming presence that, when she looked up to see his face, had her swaying on her feet.

"I think I need to sit," was the last thing she said before darkness took her.

6

THE WITCH REMOVED THE DREADED THING MAKING HIM A vampire's slave, and Dracin should have felt relief. And he did, only... something strange happened while she did it. For one, he felt her magic, a warm and tickly thing that kept sliding off of him until a different kind of magic grabbed hold. If he didn't know better, he'd have said it came from him.

Ridiculous of course. He was a dragon, not a wizard. Still, when she'd started, the fluttery sensation against his flesh roused something cold, and strange. His inner dragon was oddly quiet during it all. Unlike when he'd removed his shirt and his dragon encouraged him to also take off his pants.

The moment the foreign object cleared his body he almost cheered. Fuck those vampires and their app-controlled device. Next time he saw a bloodsucker, he'd be chomping on their bones despite their bad smell.

"Where's that whiskey?" Belle reached for the glass, her hand trembling.

Before he could ask if she was okay, she began to wilt. He caught her, but the glass fell from her limp fingers and smashed on the floor. He didn't give a fuck. The witch lay in his arms, breathing but unconscious.

"What's wrong with her?" he asked aloud as if someone would reply.

His dragon did. *Needs sleep.*

She'd overextended herself helping him. Bloody hell. What was he supposed to do with her? Even if he knew where she was staying, he didn't have his truck anymore, and calling a taxi would lead to questions such as "Why do you have an unconscious woman?" and could he really in good conscience dump her while in this vulnerable state?

Fuck me. He rose with her, careful to avoid the puddle of whiskey and broken glass, carrying her past the couch in the living room where she would have fit given her small frame. However, given what she'd done for him, it didn't seem right to dump her on it. So she got his bed. *A bed big enough for both of them,* his dragon slyly pointed out.

No.

He lay her on his sheets, placed her head on his pillow, and pulled a blanket up to her chin before standing back. Belle didn't look out of place, and he resisted an urge to stroke the stray hair across her cheek. He retreated lest he be tempted.

Upon exiting his bedroom, he softly closed the door and then let out a mutter of curses. He couldn't have even said why he was so annoyed. He'd gone from despair at being captive to striking back at those who dared imprison. No longer did he have to worry about Theodore sending him to his knees in agony. He was free.

Am I?

At his dragon's query, he went out the back door, the late hour and his location meaning he could shift without issue. His dragon emerged with a bellow of happiness.

With a mighty push of his legs, he launched himself into the air, wings snapping out to catch a current before flapping.

Relief filled him and his beast. Of everything that had happened the last few days, the fact he'd not been able to shift had been the most horrifying. Shifting had been a way of life since he was young. Not that he was allowed to do it much.

His mother had told him the first time he turned into a dragon he'd only been a few months old—a shock to a wolf shifter who'd never imagined his kind even existed. She'd found him squawking in his crib, trying to flutter. According to her, he learned to fly before he crawled, which led to her being afraid to take him outside. He spent the first few years of his life a sort of prisoner, which he understood was his mother's way of protecting him. That restriction lifted when he got old enough to understand he couldn't shift in front of people, he couldn't fly too far, and no flying during the day lest he be seen.

In retrospect, he commended his mother for all she'd done. It couldn't have been easy raising a dragon alone. She'd done everything she could to protect him, he just wished he could have been there when tragedy struck. Finding the person responsible didn't make up for the fact she'd died alone.

The depressing thought led to him uttering a bugling cry before he returned to his backyard and shifted back into his human form. He entered through the kitchen door, naked and not caring. That was, until he remembered he had a guest in his bedroom with all his clothes.

He cursed silently in his head as he debated what to do. A peek inside showed her still asleep, so he snuck in and grabbed a pair of shorts before heading for the bathroom for a shower and a hard scrub to remove the stench of his imprisonment.

While they'd kept him clean with hose-downs, his skin still crawled as he remembered how he'd been looked upon as an animal.

Bet they wouldn't have been so cocky if I'd been an actual beast and there was no cage between us.

The hot needling spray had him sighing. He braced his hands on the tile wall and hung his head, letting it rinse the back of his neck, the healing almost complete. By the morning, which was only a few hours off, it would be unnoticeable. All thanks to the witch.

Mate.

His dragon just couldn't resist, and Dracin wanted to snap, only the relaxing shower had him mellow. As he ran soap over his body, he let himself think of her. That mouth, perfect for kissing—and cock sucking. The very thought of her on her knees, looking up at him, her lips parted to take his shaft...

A shudder went through him. Fuck, he was suddenly horny. He grabbed his engorged cock with a soapy hand, sliding back and forth along his length. Usually when he jerked off, he did so methodically. Pump it fast and eventually he would come.

But this time, his mind wanted a visual, and it chose Belle, astride him, naked. He imagined her tits bouncing as she rode him, her fingers digging into his chest. Her hair spilling around her shoulders. Her lips parted as she panted.

It was so real—and titillating.

As he fisted faster and faster, his breathing quickened, and his hips jerked in time. He didn't understand how he could picture her as his lover so easily. He couldn't even be sure what kind of body she had, given she'd worn a jacket the entire time. The Belle he imagined had a wanton side to her, riding him with wild abandon, keening her pleasure as she came atop his cock.

Oh fuck, yes. With a grunt, he shot his load, the cooling shower sluicing it down the drain.

Hot damn, that was intense. As the water continued to grow colder, he shook off his languor and stepped out. Briskly towelling off. Sliding on his shorts. He exited to see his bedroom door open.

His long stride took him inside to see an empty bed, the sheets pulled up to his pillow. He whirled and listened, already knowing he wouldn't hear her inside. Her scent went to the front door and out. The crunch of gravel had him racing to the window in time to see taillights disappearing up his drive.

She'd left.

Without saying goodbye.

Nooo! His dragon didn't like it one bit.

Too bad. Dracin preferred that she'd left without forcing him to grovel and thank her. That sinking sensation? Nothing to do with the fact he wouldn't see her again. Had no idea how to contact her.

Not that he would have.

Nope.

"I'm glad she's gone," he muttered as he crawled into his bed, a bed infested with her scent. It enveloped him and followed him into sleep, where he dreamed of her and woke in a puddle of cum.

The bed got stripped and tossed in the wash, and then he scrubbed his place with a pine-scented cleaner, eradicating every trace of her presence.

Now if only he could find a way to scrub his mind.

7

Clarabelle woke in a strange bed. Feeling faint was the last thing she recalled, which led to her realizing Dracin must have tucked her in to let her sleep off her exhaustion.

She'd overextended herself. Her own fault. After the way she went after those vamps, she should have rested before attempting magic on a shifter. Then again, she'd not expected it to be so intense. The way his body reacted, almost pushing away her magic until the third force appeared. A new kind of magic latching on to her own and taking over when hers wanted to fail.

A slight sound had her holding still. The door to the room opened, and someone entered. She peeked through a slitted lid to see a bare ass not far from the bed, Dracin rummaging in a drawer. She squished her eye shut as he turned, lest he catch her spying.

The door closed, and she heard the muffled sound

of water running. He was showering. The nakedness made sense. Kind of. Why strip before grabbing clothes?

She rose from the bed—his she realized, with its plaid comforter and flannel sheets—and stretched. A glance at the clock on the nightstand, with its glowing red numerals, showed she'd slept a good two hours, enough to no longer feel lightheaded. She slipped out of the bedroom and noticed the closed bathroom door. She went past to the kitchen and dug out her phone, trying to arrange a ride back to the city. Not surprising, two a.m. in the boonies meant Uber had nothing available for this area. She grimaced. A taxi wouldn't be cheap, but she still booked one and agreed to pay a premium for out-of-boundary pickup. She doubted Dracin would want her sticking around. The ornery man's home screamed bachelor. One fabric recliner. One kitchen chair. He couldn't have stated he hated company more clearly. It was a wonder he'd had more than a single plate, fork, and knife.

The taxi arrived more quickly than expected, and she glanced at the bathroom door, still closed. She should let him know she was leaving. She'd raised her hand to knock when she heard a noise. Ear pressed to the panel, she heard a low moan.

Was he hurt?

A hand on the knob showed it unlocked, and she opened it enough to glance inside. Then blushed.

He wasn't injured but jacking off in the shower. His hand rubbing the length of his cock. An impressive cock she noted. Cheeks hot with embarrassment, she shut the door quietly and leaned on it.

The taxi waited outside. Should she hold off her departure until he'd finished?

What if he'd caught her spying?

Rather than face him, she fled.

Cowardly, she knew, and yet something about Dracin discomfited. Made her feel things she didn't understand. Lust? Since when did a man make her want sex? Sex was usually the end result when she dated someone for a while, not because of need. Yet this man oozed sexuality, and she didn't know how to handle it.

So she fled. Returned to her hotel room, where she jumped in a shower, soaping herself vigorously as if that would rid her mind of the image burned in it. His powerful body, muscled and thick, slick with moisture, his hand gripping his large shaft, moving up and down.

Who did he think of while he stroked? What did it say that she hoped it was her? *Did he think of me while he touched himself?* The very thought had her pulsing between the legs. She turned down the heat of her shower and blasted away her lusty thoughts with cold.

Still, the memory of him lingered and followed her to bed. She cast a spell on herself to sleep and woke midmorning refreshed and ready to get to work.

She now had a culprit when it came to the disappearances.

Vampires.

With everything that had transpired, she placed a call to Marjorie.

The coven leader answered. "How's it going in Ottawa?"

Without any kind of preamble, she stated, "We have a vampire problem."

A pause on the other end before Marjorie murmured, "Explain."

So she did, detailing the vamp who'd lured her to the parking garage, the cages, the fact she'd rescued a shifter but all indications pointed to him being one of many.

By the time she finished, Marjorie ranted, "Those fuckers!" It took a lot to get their coven leader swearing.

"We'll have to report the clan's crimes to the council."

"Obviously. Did you keep proof of their actions?"

"No, and I forgot to take pictures."

"Can you go back to get some?"

Clarabelle grimaced, even though Marjorie couldn't see. "I burned down the garage as a warning to stop."

"Unfortunate, but if needed, you can testify under a truth spell. Do you think this will put an end to it?"

"Even if it did, the head of the clan needs to answer for their actions. I'm hoping to track him down today."

"Alone?" Marjorie exclaimed.

"I'll ask some of the local coven to join me." All

satellite covens had to provide aid to an attaché witch acting under direct Colony Coven orders.

"As far as I know, given their lack of skill, they'd be more hindrance than help," Marjorie pointed out.

"Anyone useful close by?"

"Unfortunately, I don't have anyone to send right now. We had a bit of an issue arise in the Midwest."

"What happened?" Clarabelle asked.

"Ancient burial ground being excavated unearthed an undead surprise. It's being handled, but that leaves me without anyone to provide backup."

"Given how I've taken out a half-dozen vamps already, I'm sure it won't be a problem. The clan leader can't have many left."

"A vampire who's selling witches and whatnot won't hesitate to break the vampires' laws on creation." A law that limited the number of vampires allowed per clan based on the population size of the city they lived in. The largest clan in the world only had fifty members because their heavy eating habits, along with their rules on not killing their food, meant they required a rather large stable of blood donors.

"While you raise a valid point that he might have more lackeys than expected, I also don't recommend we wait too long to act. This Theodore will either relocate or destroy the records."

"You think you can find some of the victims?" Marjorie's question was ripe with hopeful curiosity.

"Some of them would have been bought as exhibits. So, yes, I imagine some will be alive."

"What of this shifter you saved? Think he could call in a few buddies from his pack to act as backup?"

She didn't get the impression Dracin liked asking anyone for help. Still... "I could ask. He might be willing to help, given what they did to him."

"Send me a full write-up on everything you found. I'm going to forward it to the Vampire Council to show justification for our actions. It would help if you could get a truth-verified statement from the victim you saved."

"Are you worried my testimony won't be enough?" Clarabelle didn't hide her surprise. While the vampires kept to themselves, they'd long had an understanding that, if not friendly, was amicable.

"I'd prefer if we covered our asses. We don't know if this operation was limited to Ottawa only."

"You think another clan might have been helping?"

"We don't know much at this point, so I'd like to be careful before we accidentally start an all-out war. As it is, they'll grumble that you killed them without a trial."

"Firstly, I am highly ranked enough to invoke the Dracula treaty clauses. And second, I had no choice," Clarabelle huffed. "I am allowed to defend myself."

"I know that. But let's ensure we cover all our bases. Get me some irrefutable evidence."

"And if I am attacked again?"

"Then do what you must. I'll handle the fallout."

Clarabelle hung up and gnawed her thumb. Marjorie had made her task more difficult. While the treaty made it clear that any vampire or clan caught breaking the rules could be culled without trial, there had to be just cause. Last night, she could claim self-defense. But if she went hunting down the rest of the clan, especially the leader, then she'd better make damned sure she had some damning evidence before she set him on fire.

She glanced at the time, almost lunch. A good time to go vampire hunting since they'd be hiding from daylight and at their weakest, only she'd promise Marjorie she wouldn't go alone. A reasonable request seeing as how Marjorie made a good point that this clan hadn't been shy about breaking laws. Would they have respected the one about size? She couldn't help but recall the almost feral nature of the ones she'd killed. Vampires that should have been culled for losing their cognizance. Their very existence made it likely they had greater numbers than expected.

Backup would be wise. What she didn't like? Having to go to Dracin for help. She'd kind of hoped to stay away from him given the confusion he caused within her.

It occurred to her as she dressed she didn't know how to contact Dracin. They hadn't exactly exchanged phone numbers or last names. She did have an address though, which led to her searching on the internet to see if she could find anything. She came up empty.

The man lived like a ghost. Nothing showed under his address. The name Dracin didn't do much good either. A good thing she had friends who could dig deeper. A phone call later and she had a picture of his driver's license, Dracin Smith. Age thirty-six. Single, which she'd already guessed. With that information, she made a second phone call that resulted in his identification being run against the police database. No infractions came up except for one a few days ago. Vehicle parked longer than allowed on a city street, which led to it being towed.

It gave her an idea.

A few hours later, and several hundred dollars poorer, she drove the old Ford truck to Dracin's place conscious that night fell, meaning whatever plan she'd put in motion against the vampire clan would have to wait until the next day. Never go into their nest at night when they were strongest.

She rehearsed what she'd say when she saw Dracin.

The Colony Coven for North American witches would like your aid in locating the vampire clan conducting themselves in a way that is against the current treaties forbidding the enslavement of sentient people and creatures. The most professional approach and probably not the best one.

Hey, so want to go vampire hunting? Direct, he'd probably prefer that.

The truth? *The boss witch says I can't confront the vampires by myself and wants me to bring backup.*

All of those pretty speeches flew outside her head when she pulled into his driveway to catch him splitting wood, shirt off, muscles gleaming with sweat.

He paused to watch her park, and when she

emerged, tingling head to toe and trying to ignore how delicious he looked, she blurted out, "I brought back your truck from the impound."

To which he drawled, "No shit. What do I owe you?"

"A favor."

He arched a brow. "Oh? Not sure what I can do for you."

Her mind had a dirty list, but she stuck to the reason she came. "I need you for something special."

His lips quirked. "Should I shower first?"

Her cheeks burned with heat as she realized how it might have sounded. "I mean I need your muscle."

He glanced down at his gleaming torso. "Which one?"

For some reason, she got flustered and blurted out, "All of them. It won't take long."

"Well, that's kind of insulting."

She could have died, as everything she said kept emerging wrong. "What I mean to say is I need you for backup."

The smile widened, turning a handsome man into a devasting one. "Did your batteries run out?"

"Would you stop twisting everything I say into something dirty?" she huffed, planting her hands on her hips.

The jerk laughed. "Oh, Belle, if you could see your face. Why don't we go inside and talk about this help you need over a glass of whiskey?"

She nodded. A shot of something strong might stop her from sounding like a moron.

Or not.

As his ass led the way in snug jeans, she couldn't help but remember how it looked bare. How he looked masturbating.

How she wanted nothing more than to take him up on his offer of sex.

8

SHE WATCHES.

Dracin almost looked back to see if Belle truly did stare at his ass. Did she like what she saw?

She'd certainly been blushing prettily when he'd been purposely obtuse with her requests. In his defense, her unexpected arrival had put him off kilter. He'd honestly thought he'd never see her again, then, bam, she showed up in his truck. How had she found it? He'd assumed the vampires disposed of it.

What did it say that she'd gone through the trouble of trying to locate him? For help, mind you, but still, she could have probably asked for aid from any number of people. Why him in particular? Had she missed him?

To his annoyance, he had missed her, and he hated the fact he'd already jerked off twice today thinking of her. He couldn't get her out of his head, and now she wanted his muscle—sadly, not the muscle between his legs. She needed protection. Mostly likely from those fucking vampires. She'd better not be their next target, or else.

Eat them.

His dragon had the right idea. Still, he'd not lived under the radar by hunting blood suckers and getting involved in shit that didn't concern him. He'd escaped. The other victims? Not his problem. However, he couldn't deny he'd enjoy meeting up with Theodore and punching him until he had no teeth left.

Belle followed him inside, and it wasn't until he poured the whiskey and handed her a glass that it hit him. The scent of her arousal. Holy fuck, the blushing was about more than the verbal play on words. The way she avoided looking at him? She liked what she saw.

It led to him not putting his shirt on. Playing dirty? Yup, and he was okay with it.

He'd never been more aware of the fact his antisocial nature left him with only one chair in the kitchen, which he offered to her while he stood leaning against the counter, sipping his drink. "So, what do you need my muscle for?"

Her cheeks turned pink, and the perfume of her lust almost had him hitting his knees begging for a taste.

"My superior has requested I find backup before confronting the remaining vampires in the Ottawa-based clan. Given the local witches aren't at a level that can aid me, it was suggested I speak to a shifter. AKA one that has a vested interest perhaps in ensuring those responsible for his incarceration pay for their actions."

"You want me to kick some ass."

"More like support me while I handle the execution of the vampire in charge as well as retrieve any evidence that will satisfy the vampire council of their guilt and possibly lead to the recovery of other victims."

He raised a brow. "Just that?"

She shrugged. "The latter parts are more for me to handle. You and whatever pack friends you choose to invite will be there more to ensure I'm not surprised in case there is more opposition than expected."

"I don't have a pack."

"Oh. Sorry. I just assumed, given you're a shifter, that you would belong to one."

"Nope. No real friends either."

Her lips pursed. "That's unfortunate. I guess I'll have to contact the local Alpha and see if I can borrow—"

He cut her off. "You don't need them. I'm worth ten of those furballs on a bad day."

"Isn't the F word considered derogatory?"

"Maybe to them." He shrugged.

"But you're one of them."

It hit him then. She still had no idea what he was.

She thought him some kind of mangy dog. Hell, he and his mom thought for the longest time he was the only one until he happened to encounter another dragon in the sky during one of his night flights. Excited to finally meet someone like him, he'd bugled a greeting. It resulted in the other dragon attacking him. He'd barely survived. As for the other dragon... the mangled body, back in its human shape, had no clues to offer. Hence why he'd stuck to his mother's advice—*Tell no one what you are. Stay away from the pack.*

Belle waved a hand. "Doesn't really matter what your animal is. I know you're tough."

Yes. I am. His dragon preened.

"Do you know where to find Theodore and the rest of his gang?" he asked, sipping his whiskey.

"No, but I have the resources to track him down."

"Exactly who are you?" he asked, setting the glass down and heading for the fridge. He'd not had dinner yet, given he'd been splitting wood for the coming winter. His wood stove went through at least three cords per chilly season.

"Clarabelle Montgomery."

"I know your name. I meant who, or what, are you? A witch, obviously, but you sound like you're working for someone. You mentioned a boss."

"I'm an attaché witch for the Colony Coven, which oversees all the witches and smaller covens in North America. I'm what you might call a problem solver. They send me to locations to handle delicate matters."

"I'd hardly call the vampires and their trafficking delicate," he stated, pulling out the butcher-paper-wrapped steaks. "You eat meat?" He held it up in question.

"Yes." She cocked her head. "But not a large portion. And I'll take a vegetable on the side if you have any."

He chuckled. "Not many of those around here. I'm more of a carnivore, but I do have some rice."

At her nod, he went and pulled out a flavored version that wouldn't take long to cook. As he prepped the steaks, he had more questions. "Have you always been a witch, or is it something you go to school for?"

"In my case, I was always special, but I didn't learn at a young age because my parents had no idea what was wrong with me. It was assumed I intentionally set fires and caused chaos because of my troubled nature."

He glanced at her over his shoulder. "Troubled by what?"

"By the fact I could light fires when angry and toss objects around, but no one believed me when I said I wasn't actually doing it."

"But you were."

"I was, but at the time, I didn't realize I had magic. To me, the spontaneous eruption of flames was terrifying."

"So what happened?"

"I was institutionalized, and thankfully, one of the nurses on staff, a witch of modest power, recognized my ability and had me relocated."

"In other words, a Harry Potter moment?"

Her low chuckle tightened his groin. "In a sense, although our school wasn't anywhere close to as magical and wonderful. Although, given I had to sever contact with my family, my orphaned ass lived in some pretty crap places."

"Didn't any of the witches take you in?"

"In a perfect world, I'd have lived in a lovely Victorian, with a wise old woman who would impart knowledge as we stirred a cauldron together. The reality is nobody wanted to deal with a powerful teen witch with an unpredictable temper."

"I get it. I went through a phase where my anger issues led to me not always being in control. But in my case, I had my mom to slap some sense into me."

"She beat you?"

He rolled his shoulders. "Not in a mean way. Keep in mind, shifters are volatile by nature. Talking and stuff is all nice and good for humans. Their kids can't shift and tear out the throats of those annoying them. So, yes, my mom smacked me when I was bad. When I got larger, she resorted to a solid wooden spoon." He turned and couldn't help but smile as he remembered, "When I got way taller than her, she used to stand on a chair to give me my rebuke."

"And you let her?"

"She was my mom. I'd have never laid a finger on her." He'd been crushed when she died. Almost took his own life in his grief because the loneliness had been so utterly devastating.

"I don't remember my parents other than the fact they hated me. They were deeply religious and convinced I was a Satan-loving demon."

"Ouch."

"They weren't entirely wrong. The Dark Lord is who I pray to." Said matter-of-fact and he blinked.

"You worship Satan?"

"How do you think I got so powerful?"

He stared at her. "But you're so cute." The words spilled from him.

Her cheek dimpled when she smiled. "Ah yes, because Satan's witches should be hideous."

"I've seen the cartoons. You're supposed to be green with a wart and hideous straw-like black hair."

Her laugher froze him, mostly because he enjoyed it so much he forgot about his steaks on the stove. He whirled to quickly flip the steaks as she chuckled. "Sorry to disappoint. If it makes you feel better, I ride a broom. Which reminds me, where do you keep yours? I had to call a taxi last night because I couldn't find one."

"Just inside the basement door. There's a mop, too, if you need one." The inanity of the statement almost had him shaking his head.

"Excellent."

"You don't need to fly, though. I can drive you wherever you need to go, now that you've returned my truck."

"Appreciated. I might take you up on the offer once we're done plotting. I brought my computer so we could begin our search for the clan nest tonight."

"Witches use computers?"

"Yes, and indoor plumbing. We use electric mixers instead of stirring cauldrons too. We're quite modern you know."

"Sorry. Guess I should keep my mouth shut." He plated their steaks and the rice that had finished heating.

Once more he ran into a seating problem, seeing as how she had his only chair. So again he ate at the counter, standing.

She took a bite before remarking. "I didn't know you could buy a kitchen set with just one seat."

"Thrift store. I bought them separately."

"You, thrift?" She blinked at him.

"I like bargain shopping," he retorted a tad defensively.

"Oh, that wasn't meant as an insult. I'm impressed. Especially since you have an eye for quality. This table and chair are solidly built and in great condition."

"They weren't when I got them. I stripped, stained, and varnished them."

"A handy fellow."

He shrugged. "Mom used to say idle hands got in trouble."

"She's not wrong. What do you do for work?"

"Nothing right now. The cabinet company that employed me fired me because I failed to show up or call in sick for a few days."

"Guess you can't exactly tell them a vampire kidnapped you."

He almost spat out his steak. He swallowed and managed a gruff, "Not sure that would have gone over well. It's fine. It wasn't a great place anyhow. I'll find something else to pay the bills."

"You should think of doing handyman stuff." She stoked the tabletop in a way that made him slightly jealous. "People pay good money for this kind of quality work."

"Problem is dealing with people."

Once more her laughter hit him hard. "Good point. And good dinner. I am stuffed." She'd only eaten half of the steak he'd given her. Not one to waste, he jabbed it with his fork when he snared her plate. He chewed it as he started filling the sink with water.

"I don't have dessert, I'm afraid," he stated as he finished the hunk of meat.

"No sweet tooth?"

Not for sugar, but a certain witch... He turned from her and tossed the empty fork into the sink.

"Need a hand with those?" she offered.

"Nah. Won't take me but a minute to do." He set up the drying rack, seeing as how he actually had dishes to wash. He usually ate out of the pan. It seemed a good time to ask, "So how are you going to find the blood suckers?"

"The boring way. By accessing the archive of vampire clans and seeing if this Theodore has a posted address."

"If he doesn't?"

"Then wander the city street and hope I can lure one out of hiding so I can use them to scry for a location."

"You are not dangling yourself as bait," he growled.

"Says who?"

"Me."

"Because you totally get a say," her sassy response.

He whirled from the sink filling with water. "Because it's a dumb risk. If you can't locate them via mundane methods, then I'll find them."

"How? You going to wander around the city sniffing every alley?"

"If necessary."

She stared at him a moment before nodding. "Very well. If you insist. Thank you for the offer."

Her easy acquiescence had him narrowing his gaze. "You were fucking with me."

Her lips curved. "If I were fucking with you, I'd be wearing less clothes." With that, she rose and headed for his living room, dragging her oversized handbag with her.

Damn…

Want. His dragon stated.

Yeah, me, too, buddy. He washed the dishes while looking out his kitchen window. The dark yard didn't have much. A scrubby patch of weeds, mostly dried and yellow with fall's crisp nights. The woods at the far end, a shadowy haven for the small creatures that oddly weren't bothered by his presence. The big predators though? They steered clear.

He'd just hung up his dish rag when the lights went out. All of the power died, leaving the house quiet.

And in that quiet, his dragon whispered, *Intruder.*

9

CLARABELLE ENJOYED DINNER IMMENSELY—AND NOT just because of the food. Dracin proved not just handy with a stove and sexy without a shirt, but he could even provide decent conversation.

As if she needed another reason to lust after him.

She left him to do dishes—which still impressed, seeing as how most guys she'd dated were more interested in dirtying her sheets than tidying a mess. She hooked her laptop to her cellphone internet via a hotspot. She'd logged onto the coven network and was sifting the listed vampire clans looking for info on the Ottawa one when the power went out. It didn't affect her laptop, seeing as how the battery remained at almost full charge; however, she still shut the lid when she heard a sibilant voice in her head, whisper, *Intruder.*

She sensed no malice and no hammering on her mental shields. Curious, she replied, *Who is this?*

The strange voice replied, *Me.*

Because that totally cleared things up. *Are you friend or foe?*

Mate was the startling reply.

Clarabelle still digested the oddity when Dracin entered the living room, not that she saw him in the dark, more like she heard and sensed. She dared not use magic to create a light, in case the voice spoke the truth and this power failure had to do with someone wishing harm.

Dracin crouched in front of her, close enough she could make out the shadows of his face and his fingers at his lips in a shushing gesture.

He leaned forward and whispered, "We have company."

"How many?"

He cocked his head before replying, "I hear six distinct voices. They think I'm alone." He paused. "They're here because they think I know where to find you."

She pursed her lips. It seemed Theodore had gotten her message and thought it a bright idea to retaliate. She couldn't help but smirk when she said, "I'm surprised they only sent six."

His teeth gleamed as he smiled. "It's because they think they still control me."

She almost laughed. Guess they'd be in for a surprise. "How do you want to handle it?"

He stood from his crouch before replying, "I'm going to say hello."

"I'm coming too." She rose, but he shook his head.

"I've got this. Stay back just in case."

Before she could argue, the alien voice spoke once more in her head, *Fun crunching.*

Wait, was that Dracin's beast speaking to her?

No time to ask. Dracin strode for the front door and flung it open, absolutely fearless when he shouted, "Come out, come out, wherever you are, you maggoty blood suckers."

From the shadows, someone hissed. "Tell us where to find the witch and you can live."

He jerked a thumb and declared, "She's inside."

Excuse me?

She might have been more indignant, but the alien voice huffed, *Safe.*

Still, Clarabelle crept over and peeked from the edge of the window.

"Step aside." The firm demand was disembodied, as the speaker had yet to step into the open.

Dracin crossed his arms. "I don't think so. And just so we're clear, you are not allowed to go into my house."

The vampire laughed. "As if we're bound by such stupid rules."

Clarabelle almost shouted, "Yes, you are." There was a specific article in the treaty that stated they could not enter a home without invitation. Part of the willing-donor stipulation.

"We are taking the witch, and you. Do you know

how many pre-bids our Lord received for those wanting to own their very own dragon?"

Dragon? Clarabelle blinked. She must have misunderstood.

"You can take those bids and shove them where the sun don't shine," was Dracin's retort.

"As if you have a choice." The vamp finally revealed himself, emerging from the concealing shadow of the truck, pointing his phone at Dracin. Showing off his fangs in a smirk, he tapped the screen.

Nothing happened.

The frantic tapping happened a few more times before the vamp realized what had happened and yelled, "He's not responding. Attack! Sleep bomb him, now."

That was Clarabelle's cue to emerge as backup, lifting her hand and sending out a pulse that stopped the soaring liquid-filled balloons and caused them to fall flat, well short of her target.

She might have done more, only she paused because the man in front of her grew. And grew. Grew some more and sprouted wings, snout, and scales.

You're a fucking dragon! she might have mind-shouted.

The smug reply? *Protect the mate.*

No time to debate what the fuck that meant. Vampires came flying from all directions. Six, as Dracin had stated, some of them armed with syringes, not that any managed to penetrate his armor. Powerful wings batted a pair aside. The one that soared off the roof and landed on Dracin's dragon back got flung with a single, vigorous shake. His serpentine head snapped forward, and a vamp got chomped hard enough the torso severed into two pieces.

Dracin picked up another with his giant jaws and shook his head, much like a dog with a toy. Seeing one of the vamps grabbing the axe by the woodpile, Clarabelle flicked her fingers, igniting the lone female in the group. The living pyre remembered the mantra, "stop, drop, and roll," not that it worked against the magical flames. Once realized, the vamp popped to her feet and ran for the woods, lighting up a tree with her passing. Bloody hell. By the time Clarabelle ensured the escaping vamp wouldn't cause a forest fire, the fight was over.

Six dead vamps. One impressive dragon. And a witch who pointed her finger and yelled, "Why didn't you tell me you were a dragon?" Not that she would have believed him without proof. She'd been taught the dragons died out. Hunted to extinction because of their violent nature.

Dracin shrank back down into his man shape, his naked man shape she should add. With a strength of will that almost hurt, she kept her eyes on his face.

He rolled those impressive shoulders. "You never asked."

"You knew I assumed you were a wolf."

His lips quirked. "Told you I wasn't pack."

"I figured that meant you were a lone wolf or a lion."

"A lion?" He arched a brow.

"Well, you do have golden hair."

He snorted. "Not my fault you figured wrong."

"Because you're not supposed to exist." She jabbed a finger. "Dragons have been pretty much extinct for centuries."

"Apparently not."

She couldn't help but have questions. "Was your mother a dragon?"

"Nope. Wolf."

"Father, then."

He shook his head. "Not sure what he was. Mom said he wasn't a shifter, though. He died before I was born."

"This is incredible and insane. A dragon," she huffed. She racked her brain for the little facts she knew, those not tainted by Hollywood movies. What little she'd learned didn't have much to say other than dragons were deadly. He'd certainly proven that with the vampires. "Do you breathe fire or ice?"

"No."

"Poison? Acid?"

Snort. "I'm not a cartoon."

"Can you fly?"

"Yup."

"Really?" Was it wrong she wanted him to show her?

"Yeah, although it wasn't easy learning. When I was young, I didn't have the strength for a stationary liftoff, so I used to jump off shit. Scared the crap out of my mom the first time I leaped from a cliff."

"She knew?"

"Yeah. Kind of hard to hide since I started shifting as a baby. You think baby-proofing for a normal kid is bad, try one that can climb the walls and hang from the ceiling." His boyish grin melted her heart.

"And she kept your shifter side a secret?"

He nodded.

"How did she manage that?"

"By not telling anyone. The pack had already rejected her for mating with an outsider. We moved around a lot when I was little. Wasn't easy, but she did her best. We went camping a lot. When I hit adulthood, I hated living in the city. Too many people, so I bought this place for the privacy. Been living here since."

"Wow." She had no other words.

"Mind if I go find some pants before we continue the grilling? It's nippy out."

She waved a hand. "Go ahead and pack a bag while you're at it."

"Why?"

"Because the vampires know where you live, meaning it's not safe for you to be out here alone, at least not until we rectify the situation."

"I'm not afraid. I can handle them."

"You handled six, and only after I deflected their sleep bombs. What if next time it's a dozen, twenty? Or they show up with guns?"

"Where am I supposed to go? I ain't exactly got the funds to be staying in a motel for long."

Before she even knew she'd say it, she blurted out, "You'll stay with me. My hotel room has two queen-sized beds."

He arched a brow. "I don't think so."

"Why not?"

"Wouldn't be appropriate," he grumbled.

She almost laughed. "We're both grown adults, and this isn't the Dark Ages. Men and women can share a room."

"We can't."

"Care to explain why? If it's because you snore, then don't worry. I have a spell for that."

His lips pursed before he growled, "Because you're too damned attractive."

She blinked. Not the answer she expected. It led to her gaze dropping. And... oh my.

The erection that jutted from his loins brought heat to her cheeks, and her glance went back to his face. "Um..."

"Yeah. I'm not apologizing for the fact you make me horny, but what I will do is make sure it's not an issue."

She could have offered to rent him a room on the coven dime. Could have done any number of things that didn't involve her stalking to within a foot of him and murmuring, "If we end up sleeping together, then so be it. I can't deny the fact I also find you handsome."

His nostrils flared. "It's more complicated than that."

"Why? Or are you going to tell me you don't have sex?"

"I have sex," he growled.

"And do your partners need to be hospitalized after?"

"What? No! What the fuck?"

"Well, you are a dragon, and they're known to be rough." At least, she assumed it.

"I've never hurt a woman."

Good to know, as long as he didn't lie. "Then why are you scared to share a room with me?"

His jaw flexed as if he struggled to speak before he finally muttered, "Because my dragon's got this crazy idea you're my mate."

"Oh." She had no reply. The very idea she could be anyone's anything flummoxed. She knew enough of shifters to understand what "mate" meant. It explained the alien voice in her head—mates could speak telepathically.

Despite misconceptions, a shifter could identify that someone was their mate, but they could choose not to act on it, to not mark the object of their desire. Judging by Dracin's apparent reluctance to tell her, she felt pretty confident he wouldn't be insisting on claiming her, which was a good thing. She had no intention of settling down, considering how her previous relationships all ended.

"I don't know if I'd worry about that," she finally said. "I'm not the forever type. Just ask any of my past partners."

He growled. A low menacing sound. "Don't agitate my beast with talk of your ex-lovers."

"Wow, with that kind of jealous attitude, you won't have to worry about me sleeping with you. The caveman routine went out of style a long time ago. Now, if you're done with the excuses, pack a bag, tug one off if you're feeling too horny, and let's go. I'll clean up the mess outside while you're getting ready."

He gaped at her. "You did not just say that."

"Masturbation is a normal and healthy way of dealing with lust." She should probably do it more often. Like now, because he certainly knew how to get her motor humming, especially with last night's image of him in the shower still fresh in her mind.

"I'll pack a bag and leave, but I'm getting my own room," he snapped.

"If you insist," she quipped.

While he prepared, she took a sample from a vampire, a snippet of clothing and a finger for scrying. Then she lit the bodies on fire, rendering them into ash, trying to forget the fact Dracin had called her pretty and irresistible. The thing about being his mate, though? Totally irrelevant. Not just because she couldn't imagine settling down with someone—especially a man she'd just met—but also because interspecies mating, while not exactly forbidden, was strongly discouraged. She'd not worked her ass off to get to her position in the coven only to lose it because she had the hots for a shifter.

By the time he emerged, the bodies were gone with

only singe marks and ash left behind. He had a bag in one hand, a broom in the other. He tossed both in the back of the truck before saying, "Thought you might like to have one handy just in case."

What she wanted was to not keep thinking of what he'd said as he drove them into the city. She did her best not to side-eye his strong profile. Tried to keep her legs pressed to control the pulse between her legs.

When he growled, "Stop making it hard," her gaze, for some reason, went to his crotch to see if he meant it literally. He did. No mistaking the bulge. He growled.

She sighed. "This is your fault. You shouldn't have said anything. Now I can't stop thinking of sex. Which is so out of the norm for me. I don't even like it half the time."

The truck swerved. "How can you not enjoy an orgasm?"

"Maybe because they're rare."

"Because you obviously had shit partners."

She uttered a noise. "Let me guess, you think you could do better."

He glanced at her, a smoldering look that singed as he purred, "I wouldn't stop until you came." Pause. "Twice."

She shivered.

He groaned and slapped the steering wheel. "Fuck me."

"I'm beginning to think I should," her mumbled reply.

To her surprise, when they got to the hotel, he

didn't ask about getting his own room, simply asked, "What floor are you on?"

She led him to her corner suite, farthest from the elevator and stairwell, the door marked with an invisible hex against intruders. The no-housekeeping sign still hung on the knob. She let him into what seemed like a spacious room until he filled it with his presence.

His big body.

His heat.

His allure.

He dropped his bag on the second bed and stared at the window.

For the first time in forever, Clarabelle felt adrift. Unsure. What should she do? The obvious answer; deny this attraction between them. At the same time, she couldn't deny a yearning to see what it would be like. She'd been drawn to him the moment they met. Would it really hurt to get it out of her system? Sex didn't have to mean forever, and if he proved as boring as the rest, then she wouldn't have to worry.

Before she'd even realized she'd come to a decision, she got close to him, close enough she could have rested her cheek on his back.

His stiffened body showed his awareness of her.

She whispered, "Is it crazy that, with everything going on, I want you to kiss me?"

He whirled and loomed, but she didn't feel any fear, just tummy-tingling excitement.

"I don't know if I can stop at a kiss," his sexy admission.

"Then don't." She reached for him, but he was so tall that he ended up palming her waist and lifting her for a kiss.

What a kiss. It meshed their mouths intimately. Slid sensuously. The tease of some tongue stole the breath. She wrapped her arms around his neck as he carried her to the bed and sat, sitting her in his lap, the hard pulse of his erection pushing against her.

She turned in his lap to straddle, and he groaned as she rubbed against his hardness. "Why can't I resist you?" he growled.

Heady words. She cupped his cheeks. "Because, right now, we're seeing each other as the forbidden fruit. It makes it more tempting. So let's get it over with and ease the sexual tension."

"You really think that will work?"

"I do." She ignored her sudden doubt in favor of the heat racing through her veins. A shiver went through him when her lips traced a line down his throat. He swallowed hard when she pushed him down on the bed and lay herself atop him.

They both wore too many clothes. Her hands tugged at his T-shirt, and he helped her to shed it then her top. The bra went flying next. He hugged her close for a kiss, her breasts pressing against his warm and naked chest, her nipples crazy sensitive and hardening at the touch.

A groan escaped him when she sucked on his tongue. Another moan rumbled when she gyrated against him, indulging in that pressure between her legs.

His hands braced on her hips, helping her to rock, though their jeans caused mutual frustration and titillation. Even with those layers, she throbbed. Hungered for more.

His fingers slid inside the waistband of her pants, teasing her flesh.

She pushed up and sat so she might unbutton them, but stopped when she caught sight of his smoldering gaze on her. Her face, not her breasts. It made her suddenly shy.

"Fuck me, but you're perfect," he growled before arching up enough to grab the tip of a nipple with his lips.

She sighed as he sucked and teased, all the while grinding against him.

When he bit down lightly, she gasped, and her body went rigid with pleasure. Coming with her pants still on!

He rolled her onto her back and covered her, his heavy body a new sensual delight.

He kept playing with her breasts, licking and sucking, teasing as his hand worked her pants down, freeing her for his touch.

And touch he did, his fingers dipping into her honey to stroke her clit, rolling her tiny orgasm into another round of building tension that had her panting.

Squirming.

Wanting…

He slid down her body and buried his face between her legs, and she keened. The stroke of his tongue against her making her body arch.

He pinned her down and lavished attention on her sensitive spot, teasing her to the point of almost screaming. Only then did he cover her and growl, "You still sure?"

"Don't you dare stop now!" She dragged him to her for a kiss, tasting herself on his lips, gasping again as the thick head of him pushed. He filled and stretched her, pausing once he'd sheathed himself.

She wrapped her legs around his hips and wiggled.

It was all the invitation he needed. His body rocked against hers, thrusting and pounding, hitting a sweet spot she'd never known before, a spot that quickly sent her over the edge, clawing his back as she came.

And kept coming.

When he groaned and stilled, she knew he'd found his own release, but unlike other lovers, he didn't shove off. He held her close, cradled against him, his cock inside her, their racing hearts and glistening flesh molded together.

"I guess you weren't kidding before about the double orgasm."

He chuckled. "And here I was going to apologize for being so fast."

"I don't think I could have waited," she admitted. She'd been overwhelmed with passion.

"I'll take it slower next time."

Next time? She might have replied, only he rolled them over, tucking her into his body in a warm cocoon, the intimacy of it new, and nice. More than nice. It felt right, which might explain why she fell asleep in his arms.

10

Dracin woke with Belle in his arms, and he had to hold in a sigh. So much for not getting involved. From the moment she'd shown up at his house, he'd been on tenterhooks, seesawing between pleasure that she'd returned—with his beloved truck!—and fear. A fear that his bachelor days were over.

But would that be so bad?

He wouldn't deny the loneliness that sometimes hit. He wouldn't deny a part of him would like to share his life with someone he didn't have to keep secrets from. Until recently it seemed impossible. Then along came Belle, an actual witch, who didn't run screaming at the sight of his dragon but rather oozed with awe—something the damned beast was still smug about.

His dragon, enraged that vampires would dare to not only show up at their lair but threaten Belle, proved to be more savage than usual. He'd never killed anyone before. In his mind, animals didn't count. Yet, those vampires attacked, and he didn't hesitate. He even bit one in two! And it didn't frighten her one bit. On the contrary, she approved. At the other end of the spectrum, he couldn't help but admire her own toughness and the fact that she didn't hesitate to act when in danger.

When she'd offered to share her hotel room, he'd tried to refuse. Knew he should keep his distance. But on the drive over, it occurred to him that if the vamps wanted her, then they might try to take her again. What if she were alone when that happened?

Protect, his dragon insisted. On that, his beast and Dracin agreed, hence why they had to share a room, despite knowing what would happen.

The best sex of his life.

Like, literally mind-blowing. Next level. Holy fuck, he wanted to do it again and again.

The only thing he managed to hold off on? Claiming her as his mate. Not easy, though. He'd wanted nothing more than to mark her flesh so the world would know she belonged to him, even as he suspected she'd arch a brow and have some sassy reply to that kind of alpha-male claiming.

For now, they were just lovers, and allies against the vampires, but his restraint would only go so far. Already, as she stirred toward wakening, he wanted nothing more than to run his hands over her tempting flesh. To get between her legs and greet her with his tongue. Have her sigh his name.

Or scream it...

She squirmed against him and uttered a cute noise before stilling. Not that it fooled him. He could tell she'd fully awakened and realized she lay cradled in his arms. Would regret follow? Only one way to find out.

"Morning, Belle," he murmured.

"Hi." The smallest, shyest syllable he'd ever heard.

He pressed his lips to the bare flesh of her shoulder, and she shivered. "You slept well?"

"Very. You?"

"Not bad, although I am feeling a little tense this morning." He shifted so that she felt the hardness of that tension.

"Again? So soon?" she squeaked.

Immediately, he felt bad. "I'm sorry. Are you sore?"

"No." She paused before softly adding, "I've never woken up with a man before."

He wanted to puff out his chest and strut. He also wanted to eviscerate every man who'd touched her and then made her feel less than perfect. "Morning sex can be a nice way to start the day." His hand slid down over her hip to cup her mound.

She shivered. "Shouldn't we shower first?"

"After," he murmured. "No point washing before we get sticky." His fingers slid between her thighs to find her slick already.

Her breathing quickened. "Why is your touch so magical?"

He chuckled. "Hardly. This is how it should be

between two people who are right for each other." Words he'd not meant to admit, let alone speak aloud.

"We can't be together, though. You're a dragon, and I'm a witch."

"And?" he replied, never mind the fact he agreed. He slid a digit into her sex while his thumb worked her nub.

She sighed. "We're not supposed to like each other."

"Never was good with rules," he admitted as he replaced his finger with his cock. He thrust into her, feeling her tighten.

She said nothing else, unless *Oh* and *Ah* counted. She came fast on his shaft, the shudder and squeeze of her channel milking his orgasm and leaving him limp. Satiation and happiness had him never wanting to move. It led to the realization his dragon might be right.

She's perfect for me. However, she'd made it clear she wanted nothing long-term. Could he convince her to change her mind?

After she ordered breakfast, he gave her another orgasm in the shower when he went down on her, loving how she gripped his hair and cried out. How she had to hold on to him after because her legs were wobbly.

I did that.

They emerged to find room service had left them a tray outside the door. While she picked at it, she tapped away on her laptop, looking utterly serious. He lounged on the bed while eating and watching.

At her frown, he asked, "What's wrong?"

"The Ottawa Clan. I've found a listing for it."

"And?"

"And for one, they're definitely in breach. The leader, one Theodore Beaumont, was told he could make six subjects."

"We've eliminated over a dozen," he reminded.

"I'm aware. Just like I noticed the ones we've fought were a mix of feral and not," she noted. "He seems to be turning people left and right while not culling the failures."

"Meaning he could have dozens more."

She bit her lip but nodded.

"Did you find an address?" he prompted.

"No." Her lips pursed. "Despite him being established for a decade now, it says 'permanent headquarters pending.'"

"Meaning we're at a dead end."

"Not exactly." She rose, wearing just a shirt and panties. She closed the curtains, sliding them along the track, putting them in the dark until she lit a fat candle. He got hard watching her bend over and retrieve a sealed bag from her purse.

A bag with a severed finger.

It acted as a cold shower on his erection. "What the fuck is that?"

"A sample from yesterday's attackers."

"May I ask why you took a vampire's finger?"

"I'm going to use it to location scry."

The unfamiliar word had him frowning. "What's scrying?"

"In this instance, think of it as a magical GPS locater."

"Really?" He flipped around on the bed so he could better see as she set herself up on the floor. She used a bowl from their breakfast and filled it with water. Into it, she dumped the finger, which looked rather gray. The closed curtains made sense. She didn't want it turning to ash in the morning light.

Lotus-style seating, with her hands on her knees, palms upward, head slightly back, her hair dangling down her back, she closed her eyes. Her lips moved, and to his surprise, he felt a strangeness in the air. A sensation he'd have sworn oozed from Belle to tickle the surface of the water. It roused something in him, an odd feeling like when she'd used magic on him to remove the implant.

She mumbled faster, and the surface of the bowl shivered with agitation. Her forehead creased as she muttered, "There's a shield blocking me from seeing." She pursed her lips. "I'm going to push harder."

While unable to help, Dracin still wanted to show support, so he sat behind her, hands on her waist, which led to his dragon hissing, *Share.*

What did it mean? His body jolted and then warmed, the tingling increasing. Her tension eased, but her chanting quickened.

A glance over her shoulder showed the water in the

bowl boiling, the finger hidden by the agitated bubbles.

With a final snapped, "Show me!" the surface stilled and they saw a building, dilapidated, the exterior mostly brick.

"Do you recognize it?" she asked softly.

To his surprise, he did. "Yeah, it's the abandoned mill. Booth Board Mill to be exact. It's on the Ottawa River, right by the bridge to Gatineau."

"A perfect location for vampires," she mused aloud.

The image in the bowl dissipated and, with it, the finger. Only murky water remained.

She grabbed it and took it to the bathroom for a flush, but when she emerged, she eyed him with curiosity. "Why didn't you tell me you could do magic?"

"Because I can't."

"The only reason I managed to push through the shield and get that clear image is because you shared your power with me."

He opened his mouth to refute, only to remember the odd feeling. "If I did, then it wasn't on purpose."

"Ever had strange things happen in your vicinity with no explanation?"

Again, he almost said no, only... "There was this one time... I was working on my truck, and I reached for my wrench, only it was out of reach. My dumb ass still strained and wiggled my fingers as if they would stretch a few inches, only instead of my fingers elongating, suddenly the wrench slammed into my grip."

At the time, he'd felt like a Jedi—who couldn't replicate the feat so assumed he'd imagined it.

"Interesting. I wonder if it's a dragon trait that never made it into the history books," she mused aloud. She eyed him. "I should warn you, it's my duty to advise my coven leader of your existence."

"I'd rather you didn't."

"Why?"

"Seeing as how I'm rare and shit, and I've managed to stay secret this long, I'd rather not be blabbing it to the world. I'd hate to have to eat any lookie-loos."

"Do you eat people often?" she asked in all seriousness.

His lips quirked. "No. The vampires were my first two-legged kill. But it's an effort at times. My dragon doesn't have much patience, and when I'm threatened, or those I care about are in harm's way, he's only got one solution each time, and it doesn't matter how many times we discuss we can't just go around eating people who annoy us."

"You talk with it?"

"Yeah. Not massive conversations. His thoughts and reasoning are pretty basic. Hungry. Tired. Horny." He winked at her.

"I hope you'll reconsider me telling my superior because they have people who specialize in unlocking abilities. Like the magic thing. Could be they can teach you how to wield it."

"I'll think about it." And he would because he wouldn't deny being tempted to find out more about what he could do. His having magic had taken him by surprise.

"So now that we know where to find the vampires, the next step is to scout out the location and see how many we're dealing with. If less than a dozen, we can easily go in and handle the situation. More than that and we'll have to call for reinforcements."

"By scout, are you talking about going into the mill?"

She shrugged. "While the vampires are weaker in the daytime, and usually sleeping, they're not completely helpless. I wouldn't want to risk being ambushed by a horde."

"Why not just raze the place while they're vulnerable? It's not that hard to set a fire."

"It would be easy, but we can't assume there are no tunnels or hidden exits."

"If there's not too many, are we just going right in and taking them out?"

At her nod, he rose from the bed. "In that case, we should also bring a spare set of clothes."

"You probably shouldn't shift outside in the open," she reminded.

"Wasn't planning to. At the same time, shifting inside will depend on the size of the space. I don't exactly fit through doorways, and low ceilings are a hindrance."

Her lips pinched. "I didn't think of that. Maybe it's best you stand guard outside."

He snorted. "Like fuck, Belle. I'm going with you,

but don't worry about me being useless. I'm pretty handy with a gun, which I happened to pack."

"I'm surprised. I thought shifters considered projectile weapons to be cheating."

"Good for them. Me, I've always been aware I might not always be able to count on my dragon if shit hits the fan. As a kid, I had to learn to fight with my fists because I couldn't scare my bullies with my beast. A gun is just another tool."

"You are a fascinating man," she murmured.

Probably the best compliment he could have asked for.

It was well past noon before they finally made it to the location. They'd spent the morning looking up information on the mill, including its layout and possible exits. The fact it was on an island concerned Belle because, as she pointed out, *"It makes getting away without notice a tad harder."* The fact it had a few bridges and access points assuaged her qualms. He didn't mention the fact that, in the very worst-case scenario, he'd fly her ass out. He wouldn't let her be captured.

They parked outside the fence topped with barbed wire that prevented access to the derelict building that had been declared historic, making a few bids to renovate complicated. A few companies had started, but none ever finished, plagued by issues. He had to wonder if the vampires had something to do with the problems.

"Let's make sure no one can report your truck to

the cops later." She waggled her fingers at his truck, and he saw no difference.

"What did you do?"

"What do you see?"

"My truck. Only it's got a bit of a glow around it."

Her lips pursed. "Interesting. I've glamoured it to look like a smart car. Gave it a Quebec license plate too. Just in case anyone sees it and reports it."

He cocked his head before muttering, "My poor truck. The shame of it."

"Don't like smart cars?"

He snorted. "I don't trust a vehicle I can lift on my own."

"Fair enough." Her laughter brought a smile to his lip. "Let's go see what we're dealing with."

The fence proved no match for Belle, who pinched the wires and cut them, creating an opening for them to pass through, but she did remark, "There must be an entrance somewhere that provides easy access."

He glanced around. "You don't think they climb over the fence?"

"I doubt they'd go through the trouble of dealing with the barbed wire at the top, meaning there has to be an easier way in." One not readily evident.

The parking area they traversed showed no sign of life. No cars either. Did vampires even drive?

The mill appeared abandoned, its windows and doors boarded except for one spot. A grimy and dented metal door that stunk of vampire.

He wrinkled his nose. "I think we found their main entrance."

"Can you tell how many?"

He shook his head. "Not exactly. A lot. Definitely more than a dozen." He glanced around.

"Hmm. So not going inside then. Before I set it on fire, let's make sure we don't see a back door. I'll go left, you go right. We'll meet up in a few minutes."

"Is splitting up wise?"

"It'll be fine. The vampires aren't coming outside. Too sunny," she pointed out.

Despite his misgivings, they went in opposing directions. He stalked along the side of the building until he reached the precarious edge that overlooked the water. The crumbling stone didn't inspire confidence, and yet he craned to see the back with more boarded openings. As a dragon, it would be simple to tear those off, although the apertures might be a little too tight for him to squeeze through.

Just as he'd decided to return to Belle, he heard the distinct sound of a pistol being cocked. He turned to face the barrel of a gun being held by a scruffy individual in army fatigues, who snapped, "This is private property, mother fucker."

"Sorry. Didn't mean to trespass. I'm a historical site buff." He lied.

"Still off-limits, so git."

"Sure thing." As Dracin went to move past the fellow, the very human fellow, he caught a whiff of vampire on his clothes—and Belle. It led to him snaring the guy by the shirt and lifting him to snarl, "What did you do to my woman?"

The wide-eyed fellow sputtered, "What woman?"

"I can smell her on you."

"I didn't hurt her," the guy huffed. "Just helped carry her inside."

His blood ran cold. "Why did she need to be carried?"

The man found his balls and spat, "She was trespassing and got what she deserved."

Before Dracin knew what he'd do, the guy flew and hit the side of the wall before dropping to the ground. A bristling Dracin stalked to him and growled. "What did you do to Belle?"

The fellow tried to crawl.

A kick in the ribs put a stop to that. Dracin loomed over the fucker and snapped, "I won't ask again."

"Put her to sleep and took her inside," the fucker finally admitted.

Dracin lost it. He grabbed the guy, lifted, and tossed him over the retaining wall into the rough Ottawa River, the current sucking him down. As if Dracin cared.

Belle was inside. Asleep. Vulnerable. Amongst monsters.

He couldn't have controlled himself if he tried. His clothes shredded as he burst out of them, his massive dragon just as panicked—and enraged.

Took our mate.

Never mind she'd not been marked. She was his in

every other way. And she needed his help. Since his size wouldn't fit through a door or window, he headed back to the rear and the old loading dock with its massive opening to move cargo in and out. Rusted shut. Locked.

Didn't matter. He dug his claws into the roll-down door and pulled, the squeal of metal satisfying even as it warned those inside. He tore it free of its moorings and tossed it into the river with a roar.

He entered a massive space, stripped of everything that used to make it a mill so it could be turned into a cesspool of bodies and graffiti.

The sunlight that spilled in illuminated enough of the dirty floor for him to see the place filled with chairs and couches that looked like they'd been dragged in from the dump. Lolling on them were drug-addled humans, who he ignored in favor of the hissing he heard from the deep shadows at the far end.

The vampires hid from the sunlight. Waited for him to step in far enough they could attack en masse.

As if he'd be so stupid.

He coiled his legs and jumped, heaving himself high enough to reach the windows overhead, blocked by plywood, an easy thing to punch out. He gripped the sill and dug in his back claws while he systematically brought light into this dark and evil place.

It served a few purposes. One, it kept the vampires from attacking him. Two, it should keep them distracted enough they'd leave Belle alone—or so he hoped, considering he'd yet to see or scent her. Third, it would cleanse this city of the foul creatures that thought they could feed on defenseless humans.

Sunlight spilled in, chasing away all the shadows and some of the vampires to keened, emitting high-pitched screams as their skin began to smolder. Others did their best to cover their faces and run for a set of narrow stairs going down.

He hesitated before following, his high vantage point allowing him to scan the entire room. There was nowhere for them to hide a body. Belle wasn't on this floor. He dropped down, and the drugged humans, those alive at any rate, barely reacted to the presence of a dragon except for one who blabbered, "Eragon, take me away," then giggled.

Dracin wouldn't fit down the stairs as his beast. A naked man with no gun would stand no chance against the fanged. But what else could he do?

He flipped into his fleshy man shape, the chill of the place almost making him shiver. He pounded down the stairs to find himself in another stripped room. The ceiling was low, but the space was wide enough he could shift, only there was no one there. The vampires who'd fled had disappeared. Their tracks led to a door, new looking, solid, metal, and embedded in fresh concrete.

Maddening but not as maddening as the fact he scented Belle. She'd gone through that portal!

He shifted quickly and began trying to tear it from its hinges, but his claws screeched something horrible on the metal. Since he couldn't rip it free, he resorted to pounding, denting, and slamming into it, but they'd built it to last, unlike the rest of this place. Chunks of the ceiling began to fall, a huge piece hitting his tail and drawing a hiss.

It didn't stop him from trying to demolish his way through. He might have succeeded, too, if someone didn't toss a Molotov cocktail into the basement with him. The bright flames that erupted were just the start of the inferno. More smashing bottles followed, the alcohol and its fire spreading and licking at the concrete. The heat and even the smoke were not the real issue. He could handle it better than most in his dragon form. The ceiling concerned him, though, as the fire didn't stick to the floor. It climbed and destroyed, and an already delicate ruin groaned.

Time to go.

No.

We have to. If he were crushed, he wouldn't be able to help Belle.

He fled, shifting shapes at the stairs, pounding up them just in time, as part of the floor collapsed into the basement, the whoosh of dust, smoke, and heat singing his backside. The junkies on the main level barely seemed to notice or care, but he tried to help, yelling at them to leave. Some roused enough to go; some didn't.

He wasn't risking his life for them.

He slammed through the only unbarricaded door and emerged into the sunlight, conscious he was naked and that the occupants in the condo across from the mill could see him if they looked. Nothing to be done for that but sprint to his truck, which had his pants in the backseat. He wasted time pulling them and a shirt on before jumping into his vehicle and slamming it into Drive. He managed to leave the secluded area before the sirens screamed past.

Left without his Belle.

But worse, with no idea how to find her.

11

It took all of thirty seconds outside the abandoned mill for Clarabelle to realize this likely wasn't the vampire clan's headquarters. For one, vampires hated being too close to water, and secondly, no leader interested in clout would live in such a dump.

At the same time, despite the fence, signs of habitation appeared all around. Recent garbage comprised of fast-food wrappers and coffee cups littering the ground. The scent of exhaust lingering on the weedy pavement with clumps of it crushed by traffic. Then there was the overall stench of blood and rot, a sure sign of vampires, and judging by what she saw, most likely the feral types they'd been encountering. Not a place anyone should enter if they valued their lives—and wanted to avoid bloodborne illness. Ferals had been known to cause infection, hence why the protocol to eliminate involved fire.

The exterior of this building appeared to be mostly brick and stone, but she doubted the inside would be fireproof. Not to mention, the plywood over the openings would burn nicely.

As she wandered to her side of the building, she couldn't help but shake her head at Dracin and his overprotective nature. She'd seen how much he disliked the idea of them splitting up. At the same time, she didn't need anyone fighting her battles or doing her job.

As she finished her inspection of the building and prepared to return to Dracin, she encountered a human. A vagrant, she thought at first, given his scruffy appearance. Unshaven, his hair a wild mess, his clothing visibly stained, and the smell... unwashed for quite some time.

"What are you doing here?" snapped the man.

"Hello, sir." She adopted a non-confrontational mien. "Perhaps you can help me. I'm looking for the owner of this place."

"Ain't no owner," he spat. "Can't you see it's a rundown dump?"

"And yet here you are, obviously guarding the location." She angled her head as her gaze dropped to the gun tucked into his waistband.

"I live here, not that it's any of your business."

"And who do you live here with?" Clarabelle questioned.

"Friends. Now git. Pretty woman like you don't want to be here when night falls."

"Why is that I wonder?" she mused aloud. "Could it be because certain vampires are using this mill as a lair?"

His brows drew together in suspicion. "Who are you?"

"Someone who needs to speak with the head of the vampires. Would you know where to find him? Name of Theodore, I believe." As she spoke, she cast a spell on the man to force him to reply. It failed, rebounding from the man's mind, repelled because of the compulsion already in place. A strong one, most likely placed by the clan leader.

"You're asking an awful lot of questions, and my boss, he don't like nosy bitches."

"No need for name calling. I simply wish for a conversation with your boss. Give me an address and I will be out of here."

"Why are you so desperate to talk to him? You know what he is."

"I do, and I also know he's not been following the rules."

The man snorted. "As if the rules apply to him."

"Where is he?"

"You want to see him so bad? Fine. We'll take you."

We? Before she'd managed to whirl, the balloon full of liquid hit and splatted her. It seemed a gaunt young woman had snuck up behind and lobbed a missile.

Stupid. She'd been careless and now paid the price. Grogginess sapped the strength in her limbs, and she had no time to even call out to Dracin before she lost consciousness.

She woke in a cage. Not the utilitarian kind she'd come across in that parking garage but one gilded in gold, situated beside a throne of the same color in a room that screamed, *I have no taste but money to spend*. Red velvet and brocade trimmed in gold braid and fringe hung in heavy curtains that draped the space and diluted the light, giving a satanic hue to everything—which the Dark Lord might approve of, but she found annoying. She looked better in cool tones.

The floor appeared to be black marble with some gray veins that must be hell to keep clean, which explained the people on their hands and knees polishing. Naked men and women, young and beautiful and human, most likely.

To her relief, Clarabelle still wore her clothes and appeared unharmed. No bite marks on her wrists. Given she still wore a belt, she didn't drop her pants to check her inner thigh, another favorite nibbling spot. A quick palpation of her neck showed no sign of chomping on the parts she could touch. A collar impeded her search.

She tugged at it, but it didn't budge, nor could she find a clasp. The true panic set in when she tried to access her magic and found it gone. That chilled her to the bone because that could only mean one thing: the ring around her neck? Circe's Collar. An ancient tool used to subdue witches.

How had the vampire leader gotten his hands on

one of the rare artifacts? Popular during the Inquisition years, they'd been gathered by the High Coven—the one situated in Europe from which all other covens sprang—and kept under heavy guard, along with other dangerous artifacts. It chilled her to think they might have a traitor. One willing to sell the one thing—other than salt water—that neutered a witch's powers.

Her plan to confront the vampire leader and take him out took an ominous turn at the realization she could do nothing. Not even light a spark.

The only good thing? She'd not dragged Dracin into this mess. Although he probably went a little nuts when he realized she'd been taken. Hopefully, he'd not look for long or draw attention. She'd hate to see him captured because she'd miscalculated.

"The witch awakens," mocked a smooth male voice, drawing her eye to a youngish-looking man striding in her direction from a set of stairs that went upwards. He wore an open-necked white shirt and dark slacks, the fabric and cut screaming custom-tailored. He might have been handsome if not for the cruel set of his eyes and lips.

"You've made a serious error in taking me," she boldly stated, holding tight to her fear. Never show trepidation even in the face of adversity or, in this case, a sadistic vampire.

"An error? I don't think so. After all, capturing a talented witch was on my to-do list. The one I currently own isn't capable of much." He waved a hand to a woman who'd been following him. At his gesture, she knelt, head bowed, her brown hair a curtain across her face. "About all she's good for is sleeping potions. She can barely locate other weaklings like herself, and she didn't even know we had a dragon in our city."

"If she's so useless, why keep her?" Clarabelle queried.

"Because it amuses me. Also, she was helpful in making enough witches disappear to draw your precious coven's attention. I was delighted when I heard they'd sent someone of much greater strength to investigate. Stronger than even I had anticipated. Impressive how you took out my minions in the garage and then at the dragon's abode."

"I'll kill you too," she promised.

He arched a brow. "Brave words considering you're in a cage under my complete control."

A tug at the collar led to her coolly asking, "Where did you get this?"

"At an auction in Europe. Although, originally, it was covered in glued jewels to hide its true purpose. A good thing I'd done my research and saw past its gaudy exterior."

A slight relief that he'd not gotten it by bribing the coven, but more disturbing... "You intentionally sought out Circe's Collar?"

"Oh yes. Imagine my delight when I came across mention of it in the diary of someone alive at that time. Created by the Inquisitors in the sixteenth century, they were the only way to separate a witch from her powers. But the really interesting fact is that power can be tapped by another witch. In this case, one that's more in tune to my demands."

It chilled Clarabelle to hear that tidbit because she'd not known of that. This wasn't good. "Are you the leader then of this clan?" Might as well confirm while he bragged.

"I am. Theodore Beaumont, your new master."

"Not for long. The coven knows of your misdeeds, as does the vampire council."

"The council is comprised of fangless old men and women who won't do anything for fear I'll come after them. For people who've lived centuries, they are very much fearful of death." Theodore didn't conceal his disdain for his peers.

"What are you planning? Why do you need magic?" She might not see a way out at the moment, but that didn't mean she wouldn't try. When she did escape, best she did so well informed so as to stop him.

"It is long past time we emerged from the shadows and took our rightful place as leaders. For far too long we've cowered from humans. The shame of it. Letting cows run the world." Contempt curled his lip. "Unlike my brethren, I am not afraid to fight, to put the humans in their place, kneeling at our feet."

"You're insane. The humans outnumber you immensely. They will kill you." It was the reason why the coven and other nonhumans had so many laws and rules when it came to keeping their powers, and differences, a secret. To prevent their discovery and another Inquisition by humans.

"I'll admit the cows can be trigger-happy, but they are also self-serving cowards. Threaten them enough and they will fall into line. Hence why I'm building an army of shifters under my complete control. Unlike witches, whose magic can mess with the implant, they are barely more than beasts and perfect slaves."

"There aren't that many shifters in the world," she pointed out.

"A good thing human mercenaries are easily bought. And then there's the many weapons that money can buy. For everything else..." Theodore offered a cruel smile. "I'll have your magic to wield."

He truly was devious.

"If you're building an army, why auction off the cryptids you've captured?" If he wanted to talk, let him spill everything.

"How else am I to raise the funds? The irony is the humans who are showering me with wealth have no idea they will die first. Every one of their purchases is still under my control. When I give the command..." He snapped his fingers. "Their temporary owners will die, and my slaves will return to serve me."

The very insanity of his serious plot had her realizing she'd gravely miscalculated. This was more than just a case of trafficking and a vampire breaking the rules.

"You won't get away with it."

"But I already have. Everything is going according to plan."

"Is it? Because it seems to me like you lost a good

chunk of your vampires, and I know, for a fact, they won't be easy to replace." In the movies, they made it seem like transition happened easily. In reality, most attempts failed and the person died. Then there were the ferals, with only a slight few managing to maintain their cognizance into their new undead life.

His lips pinched tight. "Like I said before, I underestimated you. I expected you to be soft, not a warrior who would kill. But now you're under my control, and soon, the dragon you freed will be too. I expect he'll come sauntering in soon enough, looking for his witch."

She snorted, more to ensure he didn't see the fear in her that he might be right. "Why would be come after me?"

"You've been together since his release. At this home, your hotel, then the old mill. Seems to me, he's got a vested interest in you."

"Because I paid him to be my bodyguard." She lied. "He had no interest in helping until I offered him dough and a chance to crack some heads. Now that I'm not there to pay, he'll lose interest."

"I guess we'll soon see."

With that smug declaration, the vampire left, leaving her to pace the small cage, trying to think. Her options appeared limited. The bars of her prison too thick and solid to bend. The lock on the outside not something she could pick without tools or her usual spells. To use magic, she had to remove the collar, which, ironically, could only be removed with magic, AKA another witch.

Her gaze slewed to the one who'd been kneeling on the floor. She'd moved from her spot when Theodore departed, and now browsed a table laden with food.

"Hello, I'm Clarabelle. What's your name?" she called out.

The woman at first didn't reply, although one of the servants scrubbing the floor near the witch did give Clarabelle a side-eye—and got scolded by the witch. "Don't be shirking your duties."

Clarabelle's stomach sank. Those weren't the words of someone upset with their circumstance, but still, she had to try.

"Hi, I know you can hear me. He's gone now. We can talk. Maybe find a way out of this mess."

The witch, not as young as suspected, finally slewed a gaze her way. "Who says I want out?"

"Because you're a prisoner," Clarabelle pointed out.

"Not really. Do you see a cage? My lord values my service."

"Your lord?" Clarabelle sputtered. "You only have one Lord, the dark one, and he won't be pleased to see you using that name for another."

"Ah yes, Hades, who's spurned me at the All Hallows' Eve orgy because I am not pretty or young enough to suit him." Her lip curled. "The Dark Lord who barely gave me enough magic to call myself a witch."

The bitter words made it even less likely she would

help. Still... "Do you really think allying yourself with the vampires will end well for you?"

"You heard Theodore. He's going to give me power to wield."

"No, he's going to steal mine. You'll just be his puppet," Clarabelle snapped.

The woman shrugged. "And? I'll still be his witch. Untouchable. Important." She lifted her chin. "He's promised me a place in his court."

"Until someone more useful comes along," spat Clarabelle. "He's using you."

"And aren't you trying to do that now? We both know you were going to ask me to release you. The answer is no by the way."

The reply had Clarabelle shaking her head. "Then you will not be spared when they come to rescue me."

"No one's coming. No one knows where we are. Theodore is too clever."

"Thought every despot before being taken down."

"You'll see. And you'll pay," huffed the witch. "You don't need to be pretty or even have all your limbs for the magic to work."

With that threat, the woman stalked off, kicking another mopping servant as she passed. A soul so lost in her bitterness she couldn't fathom being wrong.

Clarabelle would feel no pity when she killed her.

The first servant she'd kicked approached the cage, holding out a plate of food. "Are you hungry?" lisped the young woman. Barely past her teen years. Her gaunt frame showed she'd not been eating enough to handle the blood taken from the various puncture marks on her body.

"Thank you." She reached through the bars for the plate. Keeping her strength up would be important. "What's your name?"

"Beth."

"I'm Clarabelle. Have you been here long?"

Frail shoulders lifted and dropped. "Hard to tell. A while, I think."

"Do you have a way to get a message outside?"

Beth shook her head. "We aren't allowed to go anywhere but this room and where we sleep."

"What is this place? Do you know where we are?"

"No idea of where, just that it's a big house and this chamber is underneath the basement. The Lord had it specially built."

Meaning no windows and no easy exit. Not that Clarabelle would let that daunt her. "I'm going to escape, but I might need help."

"I'll try, but I don't know what I can do," Beth admitted, sounding chagrinned.

"Don't give up hope for one. Where there is a will, there is a way." Because she wasn't about to let some bitter, angry witch and an egomaniac of a vampire run roughshod over the world. Not to mention, she refused to be bested by the likes of them.

She would find a way out.

Somehow.

12

After escaping the mill, Dracin drove around aimlessly for a few hours. He couldn't go back to his place, not without at least looking. He just didn't know where to start.

There had to be a way to find Belle. He drove past the parking garage where he'd been ignobly held, which was now a burnt husk with yellow caution tape all over and a temporary fence erected all around. He got out of his truck for a sniff, hoping to find a scent he could track.

Nothing.

If only he knew a witch, he could have given them something of Belle's and have them do that scrying thing. How did one find a witch? He had no idea where to start his search for one.

A phone rang... not his he quickly realized, given he didn't recognize the bell-like chimes. It sang from Belle's bag in the footwell of his passenger seat. He pulled over and dug into the bag in time to see it say, *Missed Call* and a name, Marjorie. Her witch boss! Surely, she could help. He had to call her back.

Dracin poked at the screen and, after it informed him it didn't recognize his face, asked for a password—which he didn't know.

Fuck. How to unlock it? He knew better than to start trying to enter passwords. Smartphones tended to go into permanent lock with too many bad tries. He needed an expert in password cracking. Good thing he knew someone with just that type of skill. Not that he'd ever had to use Antonio before to hack a phone, but he did use the guy a while back to dig into his own birth records—since his birth certificate didn't have a father listed, and he'd hoped maybe a deeper poke into the birth registry and hospital records would give him a name.

No such luck, but maybe this time, Antonio would be able to help.

Antonio didn't look up as Dracin entered the shop with its eclectic mix of stuff. A pawn shop as a front, it offered a little bit of everything.

"Hey, Tony," Dracin said as he entered. The casual first name something they'd agreed upon the last time he'd hired his services.

"If it isn't the bastard." Tony looked up from his laptop to greet him. "Any luck finding your sperm donor?"

"Nah. Fucker doesn't want to be found, and I'm over it. I'm here because I need to get into a phone."

"Dare I ask whose?"

"Girlfriend," he said before adding, "She's been hurt and admitted to the hospital. I'm trying to get a hold of her mom, but I don't have her number." He held up the cell and waggled it. "Hoping you can help me."

Tony snorted. "Nice story. Don't care why you need in. It'll be a grand."

Dracin winced. "Ouch."

"My services ain't cheap," Tony retorted.

"Fine. I'll grab the cash. Can you start working on it?"

"Yup. There's a machine a block over." Tony took the phone while Dracin exited and hit an ATM, which spat out five hundred in bills then informed him he'd reached his daily limit.

Fuck.

A stroll back to his truck had him hemming and hawing before finally digging into Belle's bag. He felt like a dirty thief as he found her stash of cash. Another three hundred, leaving him two short. Now what?

He went back to Tony. "Fucking bank machine won't give me more until tomorrow," he grumbled, throwing the eight hundred on the counter. "I swear I'm good for it."

Tony ignored the cash and handed back the phone. "Afraid I can't help you."

"Why not?"

"You didn't mention this phone belonged to a witch."

"How can you tell?"

"Magic lock on the phone, which almost zapped it clean when I started playing with it. You should have warned me."

"Yeah, because going around telling people my girlfriend's a witch isn't crazy or nothing," his sarcastic drawl.

"Wait, is she seriously your girlfriend?"

He nodded.

"How do I know you're not lying?" Tony questioned.

"You don't. But I am telling the truth about her being in trouble."

"What kind of trouble?"

"The kind that likes to bite and suck blood."

Tony whistled. "She's going after the vampires? Ballsy."

"What do you know about them?"

"That there are more of them than is normal and people have been disappearing."

"Why haven't you reported it?" Dracin asked, even as he had no idea who to report that kind of thing to.

"I did. I told some local witch, who said she'd handle it."

"And?"

Tony shrugged. "And that was the end of it. Haven't seen her since."

"How is it you know about witches and shit?" Because it occurred to him Tony seemed awfully knowledgeable.

"Because I dabble in magic. Not that it gets me invited to the coven meetings. I've got too much sausage for the witch fest and not enough mojo for the warlocks." Tony snared the phone and concentrated for a second before handing it back. "I've unlocked it for you."

"Seriously? But you didn't do anything."

"That you could see," Tony corrected. "Device-breaking is my specialty. Some people call me a techno wizard, which is kind of cool but not something I can brag about. Last dude who did disappeared."

"Damn."

"Yeah. Hence why I'm careful, just like you are."

"I'm not a warlock," he felt a need to state.

"No, but you're something. I just can't tell what other than it ain't wolf. Can always tell when they come into the shop. Wet dog smell lingers."

Dracin's lips twitched. "Let's just say I like to keep my other self quiet."

"Totally cool, bro. Anyhow, the phone is unlocked, so don't lose it cause, right now, anyone can get in."

"What about the spell?"

"Easy to remove once I knew about it," Tony boasted.

"Thanks. I'll bring you the rest of the cash soon as I can."

"Don't worry about it." Tony slid the wad of cash back in his direction. "It's on the house. Hope your witch friend can do something about those vampires."

"Me too," said while pocketing the dough.

Dracin exited with the phone and hesitated. It felt hugely invasive to be using it, but at the same time, what else could he do? Belle's life depended on him doing something, but he couldn't act without knowing where to fucking go. Surely someone she knew could point him in a direction.

He swallowed his moral compass and poked around in her messages. Only one conversation had occurred in the last week with Marjorie. A word salad that had to be code because it made no sense, the most recent saying, *Going shopping today. Hope I find the shoes I'm looking for.*

For a second, he thought of texting, but he didn't want to pretend to be Belle. Not to mention, typing on tiny phones annoyed.

He went into the contacts and scrolled for Marjorie's name before dialing.

It rang only once, and a feminine voice replied, "Clarabelle, are you okay? Leanna had a vision and said you were in trouble."

Dracin cleared his throat. "Um, hi. Sorry to call, but I didn't know what else to do since Belle is missing."

A frosty "Who are you?" emerged.

"Dracin."

"Dracin who?"

"The guy she saved from the vampires."

"The shifter in the cage?"

"Yeah."

"You said she's missing. Explain."

"We went scouting a location looking for the head

vamp. She said we should split up to check the building for access points. She got taken. I tried to get her back but couldn't break down the door and then the place caught on fire and the floor collapsed and she's gone and I don't know what to do." He gushed an abbreviated version of what happened and then cringed. Way to sound useless.

"You did the right thing by contacting me. Thank you, Dracin. I'll handle things from here."

"What's our next move?"

"Your next move is to go home and stay out of the clutches of vampires. The coven will handle this."

"I want to help," he insisted.

"Listen, I appreciate any aid you've given Clarabelle. However, this type of matter isn't for outsiders."

"I'm a shifter." Not something he usually said aloud, but desperate times didn't allow for him to be discreet.

"But not a witch," Marjorie firmly stated. "This is coven business now."

"It's my business too," he growled. "Belle is my mate."

The pause on the other side took a while before Marjorie said softly, "I am afraid that's impossible. Witch and shifters can't mate. No interspecies can. It's simply impossible."

"Guess again," he growled.

"Listen, I'm sure you're feeling grateful she helped you. However, do not mistake gratitude for anything else. The coven thanks you for your aid, but now you need to leave this matter to those equipped to handle it. Good day."

With that, the witch on the other end didn't just hang up. She did something that caused the phone in his hand to start smoking. He dropped it to the ground, where it continued to burn without a flame, melting into a pile of plastic and metal.

Fucking hell.

He glared at it. So much for getting some help. And what was that crap about witches and shifters not being mates? Sure he didn't know much about witches and other kinds of folk that were special like him, but love was love, right?

Except, could he call it love? From the moment they'd met, he'd been attracted. Lusted. But he also liked her. She had great big balls of steel and smarts. So much to admire and... love.

He didn't care if she threw fireballs. Just like she didn't care he could turn into a dragon and bite people in half. He recalled once hearing that kids between shifters and non-shifters were unlikely, but then again, he'd never really seen himself as the daddy type. He'd also never seen himself mated, though.

Mated. Could he claim that even though he'd not marked her? Did a true mating need a bite?

Mine. His dragon seemed to think it didn't.

You can't fight fate. His mother's sad words when he'd asked why she'd fallen for a man who left her without a word while she recovered from birth. Surely if fate meant for them to be together, his father would have returned.

Unless he couldn't.

Would Dracin be like his mother and forever mourn what could have been?

No. He would find Belle.

He stomped back into Tony's shop and slapped the eight hundred in cash on the counter. "I need your help finding the vampire headquarters."

"That's a bad idea, bro."

"I am aware it's not the best one, but her damned coven basically told me to suck a dick. But I can't because Belle's my mate, and I am not leaving her in those fuckers' clutches longer than necessary."

Tony shrugged. "I wish I could help you, but the only two places I know with vamp activity burned down."

"If you're talking about the parking garage and the mill, then those shitholes weren't it. I've met the head asshole. He's the type to live behind a secured gate in luxury."

Tony drummed his fingers. "I can do some digging, but that could take time."

"I don't have time," he growled, bristling with frustration.

"Given she's your mate, have you tried honing in on your bond?"

Dracin blinked at Tony. "Er, what?"

"If you're mated, then there's a tie between you."

"We never made it official. And..." He paused

before saying, "I was told shifters and witches can't be together."

"Says who?"

"Head of her coven."

"I mean I've never met a mixed couple, but I'm sure it happens."

"It's not supposed to, according to Belle."

"Yeah, well, in this case, you seem pretty sure this witch is your person."

"Without a doubt Belle is mine."

"Then focus on that."

"I don't know how. You're the magic dude. Can't you scry or something?"

Tony shook his head. "Told you, my magic is weak. Good for debugging machines and unlocking phones. Not much else. Maybe one of the local witches can help."

"Do you know how to contact them?"

"Sorry, bro. Not offhand, but I can find out."

In the end, Dracin left after Tony promised to dig and text him if he found anything.

But Dracin didn't want to wait. Belle had already been in the vampire's grip for too long.

Back in his truck, he leaned his head on his steering wheel and blew out a breath.

Where are you? He growled and gripped his wheel tight before releasing it with a loud sigh. There had to be something he could do. He glanced at her bag. A dig through it didn't give him any clues, but the hat stuffed inside smelled of her, and he found himself clutching it, muttering, "Where the fuck are you, Belle?"

To his surprise, he didn't hear a reply, but his fingers tingled.

He blinked. He squeezed the hat harder and breathed in her scent, closing his eyes as he thought, *Where are you?*

The tingle hit harder this time, reminding him of when she'd scried, only he didn't have a bowl of water. Didn't matter. Inside his head, he saw an image, a house. A huge one. Mansion-sized.

Which didn't help without an address. Ottawa had tons of luxury homes.

Where?

The hat fell into his lap, the clue it gave useless without a street name. Meanwhile, he vibrated head to toe before shuddering and almost falling face-first onto his steering wheel. He panted as if he'd run a marathon.

He grabbed the hat to shove it aside, only to pause as he got the urge to go forward.

He dropped the fabric and frowned at it. Was he seriously going to take directions from a fucking hat?

What else could he do? He put the truck in Drive and rolled to the end of the street, stopping at the light before touching the hat again.

Forward. He held it lightly as he drove another two blocks before he got the urge to turn right.

And so it went, the drive taking him through the

city into one of the swankier neighborhoods, Rockcliffe Park, where the houses were big and luxurious.

It seemed crazy to think a vampire would set up here as his base of power, and yet he drove by the house in his vision. Drove by it and noted the fence all around, even across the driveway. The second pass he saw the cameras.

Getting in on foot would be challenging, to say the least.

Good thing he could fly.

The afternoon light waned as twilight rushed in. Perfect. He parked his car at a nearby strip mall, around back where no one would see the man stripping and putting his clothes on the seat. When it got dark enough, he emerged from his truck, buck-ass naked, and shifted.

He took to the sky, bugling a cry.

I'm coming, Belle.

13

Clarabelle could have sworn she heard Dracin in her head. Telling her he was coming.

Dammit.

The stupid—amazing—man shouldn't be risking himself. Not for such an untenable situation.

At the same time, her heart swelled. When he'd called her mate, he meant it. And guess what, she felt the same way. She'd never met a man who intrigued her like he did. Who made her body sing. Who made her feel protected even as he respected the fact she could protect herself.

Was it love? Maybe. All she knew for sure? She wouldn't let him die saving her, which meant she needed to find a way out of this bloody cage.

The witch, named Gloria—one of the supposedly missing ones from the local coven—had left for a few hours. During that time, Beth had brought Clarabelle more food and fed her tidbits of info, such as the fact the vampires Theodore ranked as worthy napped in the actual house overhead, the windows covered in sun shades. The less desirable weren't allowed inside, hence the mill, a place called the Barn, and another nest named the Sewer. The parking garage had only ever been a holding place for captured nonhumans. The auction itself was held in a hotel penthouse suite with the rich buyers coming to bid and then taking their purchase home with them.

"What's this space used for?" she'd asked Beth. The lavish décor, even if gaudy, seemed to indicate an entertaining space.

"Orgies and gorging," a soft reply with downcast eyes. *"He and his lieutenants feed down here. It's up to me and the others to clean up after."* Beth had pointed to the drains on the floor. *"Once a week, he also bites people to try and make more vampires."*

"How does he choose who to infect?"

"When we get too weak to feed, rather than kill he tries to change us. It will be my turn soon. I just hope I don't end up like the crazy ones." The sad downturn of her lips broke Clarabelle's heart. This poor woman, barely out of her teens, was already downtrodden by fate. She wanted nothing more than to rescue Beth, even as she had no idea of how to save herself.

A struck gong sent a vibration through the room and led to the servants throwing themselves prone on the floor, Beth included.

First to enter, Gloria, the traitor witch, head held

high, smirking in Clarabelle's direction. What Clarabelle wouldn't give to slap her.

Next, the vampires slunk in. Fifteen males and five females, all beautiful and haughty. Her heart broke at the sight of the frightened people who streamed in after, stripped of their clothes, some of them sobbing, others staring off blankly, their minds escaping the trauma. They were herded by wolves. Shifters doing Theodore's command. The clan leader entered last. Theodore wore nothing but pants, his chest bare but for a dangling pendant.

Ignoring the humans, Clarabelle counted twenty-one vamps and at least two shifters in the room. Who knew how many more were upstairs? Not great odds even if she had her magic.

The large table, laden with food earlier for the blood slaves, had been cleared. She feared why. Sure enough, a beefy fellow got nosed by the wolf in its direction. The poor naked man hyperventilated, eyes wide, sweating in fear. He might as well have poured gravy on himself. He only made himself more appetizing for the waiting vamps. The human sacrifice whirled to run, only to find himself face to face with a young woman, who cocked her head and smiled.

She only had to whisper, "Get on the table, cow," and the man obeyed, mesmerized by her command.

Clarabelle turned away before the feeding started, but she couldn't escape the slurping noises or grunts of satisfaction.

"You should watch and count yourself lucky I need

your magic, or you'd be on that table instead," Theodore stated, coming to stand by her cage.

"You're really asking to be staked. Slowly, just as the dawn rises," her reply.

"And you're asking to be punished," Theodore retorted. "But I still need you, so instead, let's show you what happens when you mouth off." He snapped his fingers, apparently the signal for Gloria to rush to his side.

He leaned close and whispered something to her that brought an evil smile to her lips.

Clarabelle's stomach sank as Gloria left and returned with a head-ducked Beth in her wake.

"Kneel," Theodore ordered.

Beth hit the floor, and Clarabelle knew he planned to hurt Beth to punish her. He must have seen on the cameras or been told of Beth's kindness.

Despite knowing the futility, she tried to stop him. "Leave her alone."

"Or what? You think I don't know you were trying to subvert her? Trying to use her to escape? There is no way out for you. And best you learn that now." He lifted his hand, a signal for Gloria, who squinted her eyes as she concentrated, a glow at her wrist showing a bracelet. Clarabelle didn't understand what it meant until the collar around her neck began to show a matching glow.

Gloria stole her magic!

A sickening lurch in her stomach had Clarabelle doing her best to breathe and not scream. Poor Beth.

She didn't beg or even whimper as Gloria pulled magic from Clarabelle, winding it in an inelegant wad of electricity. The bitch—because this was no witch—tossed it at the poor defenseless Beth.

The girl never stood a chance. Never made a sound as she died, electrocuted, her body jiggling and then sizzling as her hair burned and even her skin bubbled. Clarabelle didn't look away. She wanted to, but she couldn't, not when this was her fault. Her burden to bear.

"Anything to say now?" Theodore asked with a smirk.

She stared at him, expression bland as she stated, "I hope your death is painful, and as for you..." She turned to Gloria next. "The Dark Lord sees your betrayal and will have a special punishment in Hell for you."

"As if I'm ever going to die. My Lord has promised me eternal life." Gloria's smug reply.

The claim arched Clarabelle's brow. "That's pretty bold of him considering he knows witches can't be turned."

"What?" Gloria's expression would have been comical if Clarabelle weren't so angry.

"Ignore her. She lies," Theodore lied. "Let's take our place. Time for—"

Whatever he planned to announce got lost in the sudden thumping overhead. A banging hard and violent enough the ceiling cracked and chunks of it fell.

"What's happening?" Theodore yelled.

As the crevice in the ceiling widened, they could hear some of what happened. Yelling, screams, gunshots, but it was the sudden warm sensation that enveloped Clarabelle that had her breathing a name.

"Dracin."

He'd come for her.

An entire section of the ceiling collapsed, creating a dusty cloud and much pandemonium as the vamps found their dinner table crushed. Landing atop the mess he'd made, a dragon, big and beautiful, his dark scales taking on a reddish hue from the lights.

The massive head swiveled, and those beautiful eyes landed on her in the cage.

Belle, you are okay?

She could hear him, but no magic meant she couldn't reply, so she shook her head.

Let me handle the bloodsuckers, and then I'll free you.

He whirled to face the vampires who'd recovered and approached hissing, fangs out.

He hissed right back and attacked, his tail slashing through the air, taking out the wolf sneaking up. His wings flexed and sent vampires to his left and right flying. But it was his serpentine neck, with its long reach, that caused the most damage as he lunged and caught a bloodsucker and chomped, grinding the body until the bottom half fell. He gave the upper a bit of a chew before spitting it out.

One undead down. The others became more

cautious, whereas Dracin bugled a challenge and charged.

To his credit, Theodore remained calm, but Clarabelle didn't like the way he looked at Gloria. The witch turned to Clarabelle, wrist once more glowing as she pulled more magic.

"No," Clarabelle muttered. "No." She tried to stop the siphoning, but she had no power, no way to fight. She could only warn Dracin.

"Watch the woman with the glowing bracelet. She's stolen my magic!"

He whirled in time to get the brunt of a messy electrical ball to the head, knocking him back. Unlike Beth, it didn't kill him. He shook himself before roaring, which led to Gloria scrabbling to grab even more magic, rough tugs that caused Clarabelle to grunt and hit her knees.

Hold on. His voice reassured, but she felt herself getting weak, as Gloria sucked at her power to form a great big ball of fire.

Gloria cackled as she boasted, "Anyone want fried dragon meat?"

The flaming missile soared right at Dracin, who stood without flinching. The firebomb hit, and Clarabelle's eyes shut against the bright flash of light. By the time she could see again, Dracin stood unharmed, the table behind him smoldered, and Gloria gaped open-mouthed.

Enough of this, she heard him growl in her head.

Before the witch could try something new, Dracin

lunged, his serpentine neck stretching so that he might bite off Gloria's head. The headless body slumped, dead. She was the Dark Lord's problem now.

The relief at the witch being gone didn't last long, because Theodore remained, standing smug, most likely because of the really big gun he held aimed at Dracin. "Did you really think I wasn't prepared for the fact someone of your size might come gunning for me? After all, you aren't the first dragon I caught. I had one, years ago. Alas, he escaped, never to be seen again. Pity. A dragon would have fetched a sweet price due to the whole rarity thing. Because of that, I'm going to give you a choice. Surrender now, and you can live. Or, die. And before you scoff at my threat, you should know the bullets in this gun are custom and will penetrate your scales and explode, shredding your insides. So, what's it going to be? Surrender or dragon tartar?"

Can you tell him to kiss my dragon ass?

Clarabelle almost choked.

I'm going to enjoy eating him.

"I'd worry about indigestion," her reply.

Good thing I know a witch who's good with potions.

As if sensing he didn't strike the right amount of awe, Theodore interrupted their exchange. "I looked into you after your escape, Dracin Smith, father unknown, only son of Helena Smith."

The dragon didn't react, simply eyed the vampire. Clarabelle clung to the bars of her cage, wishing she could touch her magic not just to wipe the smirk from

Theodore's pompous ass but to handle the vamps and wolves forming a ring around Dracin.

"Funny thing, your mother's name seemed familiar to me, and I've been racking my brain trying to figure it out, when it hit me. More than thirty years ago, I visited Ottawa. I was just a young vamp back then. Newly blooded. Always hungry and looking for a snack. Given there was no clan in the city at that time, I had to hunt my own food. Lucky for me, I came across a man leaving a local hospital."

The dragon visibly stiffened.

"Rather than be grateful I'd chosen him, the man got offended when I demanded a sip of blood. Tried to incinerate me. Singed my custom suit." Theodore managed to sound affronted. "It was my first meeting with a warlock. Almost my last, but the presumptuous fool let me live because he said and I quote, 'I won't kill even one such as you on the day of my son's birth.'"

The low rumble from Dracin let her know this had to be his father, the one he'd never known because of Theodore.

"I have to say, that didn't sit well with me. That this man, a cow of a human, boasted he could kill me. Me, a lord in the making. So, the next night, I lay in wait by the hospital. He never even saw what hit him. He woke chained in the mill, his feet in a bucket of salt water. Great for disrupting magic by the way." Theodore's cold smile said this story would get uglier. "He wasn't the tastiest, but that didn't stop me from feeding. He lived almost a week, although he started begging for his life two days in. Told me he was a newly made father. That his wife needed him because her pack had tossed her for daring to love an outsider. It was touching enough it almost brought a tear."

Dracin visibly trembled, and Clarabelle spat, "You killed Dracin's father."

"I mean, technically, he died of dehydration and blood loss, but I guess some would say I was partially to blame."

"You'll pay for that." She spoke the words a bristling Dracin couldn't.

"Doubtful. I'm holding all the cards. Look around. There is no way out. Either the dragon gives up and is sold as a pet, or he dies."

"He'll kill you before he becomes a prisoner," she stated.

"He can certainly try, but here's the thing. If he's busy trying to kill me, then that leaves you vulnerable to my lieutenants." The vampires watching rustled and grinned, monsters who would gladly suck her dry. "Either way, you lose."

Dracin stamped his feet, shaking with rage, and despite the collar she wore, she saw a distortion around him, a glow that indicated magic boiled within. A magic he didn't know how to direct. But she did.

She murmured, "Remember what I did in the parking garage."

Burn? the reply from the beast.

How? the man asked.

Alas, she couldn't show him. Just whisper, "Follow

your instinct. Surely the legends about dragons got some things right."

"Quiet," Theodore barked. "Enough stalling. I want an answer. Live or die?"

Dracin stared intently at Theodore.

"Poor dumb lizard. I think I just fried what little brain he had." As Theodore laughed, Clarabelle watched as the tension in Dracin built, his body quivering, his eyes turning black, his nostrils smoking.

She clung tight to the bars and watched as Dracin's mouth opened wide and fire spewed. He missed Theodore with the first stream, but he got the vampires to the left, who shrieked as they ran, living torches with no water to douse, only alcohol in their glasses, which, when poured, spread the flames.

Theodore gaped. "This isn't possible," a quick retort before he tried to flee.

She yelled, "He's getting away!"

Dracin aimed his next fiery breath at the vampire leader, spewing hot flames that ignited everything in its path—furniture, tapestries, vampires, and the shifters caught up in the madness. Not everyone ignited. Some of the human slaves made it to the stairs and disappeared from sight. She hoped some of them managed to escape.

Smoke began to fill the room, making it hard to see, the rough grit of it making her cough "We have to get out," she gasped.

The cage she'd not been able to escape from didn't stand a chance when Dracin gripped those bars in dragon claws and pulled. She slipped out, only to pause. The fire had spread rapidly, ringing them in flames, cutting off the exit via the stairs. If she'd had magic, she could have shielded herself. But she didn't have any protection.

She pressed her face against him. "Escape while you can."

Not without you. Trust me.

She didn't flinch when the claws gripped her, but she did suck in a breath—of smoke—as he suddenly jumped, flapping his wings, spreading ash, embers, and flames as he rose above the conflagration to the ceiling, and the hole he'd smashed in it.

The smoke followed, but it wasn't as thick, and they kept rising, the destruction he'd meted on his way to find her now their escape route. They exited via the roof into a beautiful night sky, full of stars, fresh air, and freedom.

14

Emotions whirled within Dracin, a turmoil he didn't have time to fully process, even as a few key items kept forcing themselves to the surface. His father hadn't abandoned him! He'd saved Belle from harm. He'd killed the fucker behind it all.

It led to him feeling relief that the threat had been eliminated and sorrow at what he'd lost, as well as joy at what was to come.

As he flew, his precious mate in his grip, he ignored the inferno he left behind. Let it burn. Let that awful, evil place die with its master. From the moment he'd smashed his way through the many floors into that basement level, he'd been appalled at what he'd found. From a room with bunkbeds filled with shifters under Theodore's control to an actual dungeon with whips and chains and a drain in the floor, then the vampire's buffet level, replete with his sweet witch in a cage.

He wondered at Belle's calmness as they flew until

he remembered she'd mentioned before using a broom. Wouldn't it be a hoot if they both went for a flight one night?

Seeing the clearing with his house, he brought them down in a spiral. He probably should have returned to his truck, but in his rush—and anxiety to get Belle clear—he'd wanted the comfort and safety of home. He'd worry about bringing his vehicle on the morrow after he'd reassured himself Belle truly was okay. If it got impounded again, then so be it. He had more important things to worry about.

He landed in his yard and gently deposited his witch. As he shifted, he remained conscious she watched him for the second time in as many days, and despite his mother's warning, he didn't hide or fear what she'd think.

Her lips curved as he returned to his man shape. "Well, that was interesting. You really can fly."

He shrugged. "Yeah, but I don't get to do it as often as I'd like. The whole keeping hidden thing, you know."

"With your magic, I bet we could fashion an invisibility shield."

"Really?" He couldn't help but sound interested.

She nodded. "It wouldn't be perfect. Movement does tend to cause the illusion to waver, but at night, it wouldn't really be noticeable. I use it when I travel by broom."

His lips curved. "I can't wait to see that."

"Oh. Is the thought of me straddling a stick that

fascinating?" she purred, drawing close and tucking herself into his chest.

"Don't you tempt me. You need a shower and rest after your ordeal."

She snorted. "Bah. I'm fine. Although..." She stretched a finger between her neck and the collar. "I'd like to get this off."

"What is it?" he asked, eyeing the snug metal ring.

"Circe's Collar. Created to control witches. It can only be removed by magic. Which I don't currently have." Her nose wrinkled.

"Think you can walk me through how I can get it off?"

"Put your hands on it and focus your power. Imagine it unfastening the collar."

"Seems too easy. Why not use an actual lock?"

"A lock can be picked, but a witch with no magic needs help from another witch. In the Inquisition days, none would have dared to get close enough, lest they be collared too."

"Damn."

"Witches, like dragons, have been persecuted through time. It is what it is."

"It sucks," Dracin muttered as he put his fingertips on the metal, warmer than expected. He grimaced. "It's got a slimy feel to it."

"That would be the curse aspect of it."

"Let's see if I can get it to pop off," he murmured. He pressed against it, his eyes shut, trying to focus on that strange sensation inside him. A bare spark compared to the inferno of before. He grunted, "I'm a little spent, but..." He forced out the last of his juice, straining to pour it all into the collar, which he imagined splitting open.

Click.

Panting from the exertion, Dracin opened his eyes to see Belle removing it from her slender neck. She eyed it with distaste. "I don't suppose you have a box with a lock we can put this in? I'll have to get it to the coven for proper storage."

"Will a gun case work?"

In short order, they had the dreaded collar boxed away and the tub filling with hot water. Despite her protest that she could just take a shower, he insisted she soak in the hot water.

He sat by the tub with a washcloth while she relaxed. As he trailed the wet fabric over her body, she softly said, "Are you okay? What Theodore said about your father must have been hard to hear."

"Actually, he finally helped me to come to terms with that part of my life. It's kind of a relief to know Mom and I weren't abandoned."

"I'm sorry your father never got a chance to know you."

"Me too, but at least I had my mom. She made sure I didn't lack anything. I just wish she could have known he didn't run off." His lips turned down.

"She knew." She put her hand over his. "True mates can't stand to be apart."

The statement stilled his washing, and his gaze slowly met hers. "It's why I had to come for you."

"I know." She reached out to trail damp fingers over his cheek. "Even as I was mad you risked yourself to save me."

"You would have done the same."

Her lips curved. "I would have." She tilted her head. "How did you find me?"

"Magical hat." It sounded crazy spoken aloud.

She blinked.

"I might have accidentally turned your hat into a scrying woolly."

Her laughter rang out, and he could resist no longer. He dragged her from the water into his lap, not caring if his track pants got soaked. He needed to touch her. Kiss her.

He carried her to his bed, laying her atop it, her naked splendor making him want to lose control and fall upon her. But he also wanted to sensually explore.

The pleasure started with him parting her legs, exposing her sex to his gaze. She shivered.

"Are you cold?" he asked.

"No. Just wishing you'd hurry up." She rolled her hips to tease.

"Just for that, I am going to take my sweet time."

He knelt between her legs, leaning in close to blow hotly against her, making her shudder and moan. A quick lick, just one, had her hips slamming upward, almost knocking him out.

A forearm braced over her lower belly kept her in

place for his next swipe of the tongue. She could only shiver and moan as he teased her, swirling his tongue around her clit, lavishing it with attention until she panted and writhed with need.

Only then did he stop, and she uttered a moan of protest, a sound he caught with his mouth as he kissed her. A kiss that he never wanted to end. He sucked on her lower lip before slipping his tongue into her mouth for a sensual entanglement. Their ragged breaths meshed as their passion mounted, the heat between them making him wild.

He couldn't help but return to the sweetness of her sex, sliding his lips up and down her inner thighs until she begged him, "Would you kiss me there already?"

His soft chuckle vibrated against her flesh.

He began to lick again, teasing that swollen button, parting her lips to taste her honey. Her fingers threaded through his hair and dug into his scalp as she rolled with his ministrations.

She tasted sweet, perfect. Her scent drove him wild. He loved that she let herself go, the passion taking her and making her vocal. Sinking a finger into her only made him throb harder. She was so damned wet and ready for him.

His pants hit the floor, and he covered her, his lips once more meshing with hers, the head of his cock pushing. He sank into her, her sex stretching and squeezing him tight. Her legs wrapped around his shanks, urging him to go deeper.

So deeper he went, his thrusts short, as he ground

into her, knowing he'd found her sweet spot by the keening noise she made and the nails digging into his shoulders.

As her body coiled, tightening for orgasm, she gasped, "Do it."

He almost asked what.

But his dragon knew.

His lips found the soft skin at the base of her neck, a good place for a mark. As he pounded into her, her orgasm rippled, drawing his own climax. At the peak of it, he bit down, marking her as his mate, even as his heart had already known they belonged together.

Her sex clenched him tight, milking him, taking everything from him and then giving pleasure right back.

Mine.

The word came from her and him. An acknowledgement that this was forever. For however long that might be.

It turned out to be less time than expected.

15

Clarabelle slept soundly in the arms of her dragon mate. How she'd changed in the days since they'd met, going from single and fine with it to in love and more or less married. Was it quick? Yes. But that only proved the strength of their mating bond. A tie she wouldn't deny.

They woke to the sound of someone knocking. Dracin didn't seem to care and remained spooned around her.

She on the other hand... "Expecting someone?"

"Nope." He nuzzled the back of her neck.

"Could be a delivery."

He snorted. "Out here? Not to mention I don't like that online shopping shit. Most likely some desperate salesman or religious nut."

The knocking ceased and turned into someone's amplified voice. "I know you're in there, Clarabelle. Answer the door."

Her eyes widened. "It's Marjorie."

The declaration made him growl. "The woman who refused to let me help rescue you."

His reply had her exclaiming, "Wait, you spoke to Marjorie? How? When?"

"I had someone unlock your phone for me so I could get some help locating you. I called your boss, but she told me to go chew on a bone and leave you alone."

"I see you listened," her wry reply.

He shrugged. "I wasn't about to leave you a second longer than I had to with that bloodsucker."

She sighed. "And I appreciate that, but it doesn't sound like Marjorie does. I'd better go deal with her." She rose, her flesh heating as she felt his stare roving her naked body. She offered him a coy look over her bare shoulder. "I'll try to be quick."

"I'll be in the shower. Holler if you need me."

Doubtful she'd need rescuing. Marjorie most likely wanted to check on her. She threw on a shirt of Dracin's, long enough it almost hit her knees, and headed downstairs to let Marjorie inside.

The older woman entered with a huffed, "About time. I thought I was going to have to blow off the hinges."

"Or you could have simply unlocked the door. Coffee?" Clarabelle asked, heading for the kitchen.

"Yes, but it better come with answers. What the hell happened? After the shifter you saved called, I got to Ottawa fast as I could with a team, only to find the vampire leader's home in flames and most of his minions dead."

Impatient dragon. She hid a smile as she answered. "Dracin was too worried to wait."

"This Dracin wasn't supposed to get involved at all. Damned wolves never listen," Marjorie grumbled.

"He's not a wolf." The words slipped out, and she regretted it the moment Marjorie's expression changed.

"Then what is he? I thought you said you rescued a shifter."

"I did, just not a wolf." She didn't expand any further. The Keurig spit out the first coffee, and she handed it to Marjorie before making a second. "How did you find me?"

"Not easily," Marjorie grumbled. "I happened to be doing a sweep in the sky for escaped vampires when I caught a trace of magic, which led me to a truck with a bespelled hat inside, along with your bag. I had someone run the plates, which led me here. You should have called to let me know you were okay."

"I didn't have my phone." A weak excuse. In reality, she'd not been thinking about anything other than her relief at surviving and the pleasure Dracin offered.

"Start talking and don't leave out any details, because, right now, I've got a very angry vampire council wondering why their appointees for this city were killed."

"As I told you already, he was trafficking witches, shifters, and other nonhumans."

"You have proof?"

"Nothing on paper yet, but I can testify, as can Dracin."

Marjorie's lips pinched. "Are there others who can corroborate?"

"Most likely. The previous victims were sold. I don't know to who, yet. My untimely capture didn't allow me to uncover where they went. However, a forensic audit of the clan's financials should give us a clue."

"I take it you had to fight your way out, hence the fire."

"Actually, Dracin rescued me. A good thing since Theodore had a Circe's Collar."

Marjorie spat out her coffee.

While Clarabelle wiped up the mess, the coven's highest-ranked witch gasped, "What do you mean he had a Circe's Collar? None are missing from the vault."

"It wasn't stolen. He came across one that was missed." She went and fetched the box to show Marjorie, who blanched at the sight of the collar.

"Put that thing away. It gives me the shivers just seeing it." Marjorie shuddered.

Clarabelle shut the case. "I don't have the controlling bracelet. The witch wearing it—"

"Wait, he had a witch helping him?"

Clarabelle nodded. "One of the ones who went missing. She's dead, her body in the basement with Theodore and the vampires present."

"I wonder if we can retrieve the bracelet from the ruins," Marjorie mused. "The fact he had this will make our case more solid. Although it would help if we could find witnesses to his perfidy who aren't connected to the coven or involved in this Theodore's killing."

"I'm sure Dracin and I can track some of the servants and shifters he controlled. I saw some of them escaping when all Hell broke loose."

"I'm surprised you didn't stay behind to control the mess." Disapproval lined Marjorie's words and expression.

"Dracin was more concerned with getting me far away."

"More like he couldn't wait to seduce you, knowing you'd be grateful for his rescue." Her lip curled.

The barely veiled disgust lifted Clarabelle's chin. "He didn't have to try hard since we were already lovers." At Marjorie's pinched expression, she added, "And for the sake of honesty, we're mated."

"You can't be!" Marjorie's quick retort. "It's against the rules."

"What rules? I've never seen it written anywhere. It's always more been a suggestion because of the incompatibility between witches and other nonhumans, which is apparently dependent on the couple."

"Witches can't have babies with shifters."

"Not true. Look at Dracin. He's the result of a wizard and a wolf falling in love."

Her lips pressed. "He's an abomination who should have never been born."

"How can you say that?"

"Because he's a dragon."

Clarabelle blinked. "How do you know?"

"I wasn't sure until you mentioned the origin of his parents. True mated, I assume?" At her nod, Marjorie added, "The progeny of such a coupling, when successful, are dragons. The most dangerous of creatures."

At that, Clarabelle snorted. "Hardly."

"You're going to tell me he's never killed anyone?"

"Only to protect himself and me."

"For now. They're cold-blooded killers."

"Then what does that make me? Or are we not tallying those I've had to eliminate to keep the coven safe over the years?" her sassy reply.

The rebuttal had Marjorie looking pissed. "History has stories about them."

"History is often wrong, which you should well know. Look at what it says about witches."

"Most of which is true. We are devil-worshipping magic users."

"But we don't steal babies or curse crops," her retort. "Just like he doesn't go around biting people and stealing sheep."

"What about debauching virgins?"

"Marjorie!"

"What? It's a valid question, given what I know."

"No virgins. Wouldn't want the pressure." Dracin's deep voice interrupted, and Clarabelle turned to see him leaning in the kitchen doorway. His hair remained damp from the shower, but he'd dressed in a T-shirt and jeans. He padded barefoot toward her, and she tilted her head for a kiss, not caring if it made Marjorie mad.

Sure enough, Marjorie grumbled. "You know I can't condone this."

It led to Clarabelle being snippy. "Then don't. My life, my choice."

"The coven will have to be told. Once they know, you'll be demoted from your position, if not outright banned."

"For what? Daring to be in love?" Clarabelle snapped.

"Witches and shifters aren't supposed to mix." Marjorie's prim reply

"Too late," her sassy reply, which led to Dracin trying to hide a snort. He busied himself making a coffee.

"You are making a mistake," Marjorie insisted.

"Or maybe the coven needs to re-evaluate some of its long-held beliefs. You say you know about dragons, but the ones you speak of are long dead. Their supposed actions written down by a third party. And we know how that works." Distortions were in the eye of the history re-teller.

"We can discuss this more later. We have some cleanup to do, seeing as how you left a giant mess," Marjorie complained.

"I thought the fire handled the vamps."

"It did, and I've left Nexie on site there to make sure the firemen don't find anything they shouldn't. However, according to Jandy, who's been doing some digging into Theodore's records, there are at least two other locations we need to check out."

She recalled Beth's information. "The Barn and Sewer. We'll need heavy firepower, as that's where he kept the ferals," Clarabelle noted.

"Really?" Marjorie actually perked up. "Finally, some evidence that doesn't rely on your testimony. That will go a long way toward cementing our case to the vampire council."

"Vampire council, witch coven, werewolf packs. What's the organization for dragons?" muttered Dracin.

"There is none because you're not supposed to exist." Marjorie's reply.

"Or maybe we do but you don't know about us because of your attitude," his hot retort. "Ever think that maybe, just maybe, we don't want to deal with ignorance? How about you judge me for my character and not what others have said about dragons long dead?"

"I don't need to be turned to stone by a basilisk to know it's dangerous." Marjorie's prim retort.

"I'm not a monster," Dracin grumbled.

"Only time will tell." Marjorie eyed Clarabelle. "How quickly can you be ready to go?"

"We just need to get dressed and have a bite to eat," Dracin stated. "Once we're done in the city, I can grab my truck to bring us home."

"We?" Marjorie arched a brow. "You're not invited."

"Don't be stubborn. He can help," Clarabelle

insisted. "He's the one who saved me last night, on his own I might add."

"I don't know how he's planning to join us. I rode here on my broom, which we both know can't handle two people. And before you tell me a dragon can fly, I'd say he might draw attention, given it's a sunny, blue-skied day and even the best witch can't hold two illusion spells at once."

Before Dracin could say anything, Clarabelle sent him a mind message. *Don't mention you have magic!*

He pressed his lips. "I don't like the idea of Clarabelle going alone."

"She won't be alone. She'll be with me, and others from the coven."

Clarabelle put a hand on his arm. "I'll be safe. The protocol with ferals is to not even get close to them. We'll confirm their nest, seal the exits, and ignite the interior."

"And if there's a human guard like at the mill?"

"Then, when night falls, you'll have to rescue me again." She leaned up to kiss his cheek and whisper, "I'll be fine. It will give me a chance to talk to Marjorie."

He kept his misgivings to himself but couldn't hide his glowering expression. It only lightened when he reminded her the broom was in the back of the truck, meaning she had to ride a mop, the kind with long woolly strands. Her coven would never let her live it down.

Dracin held her close for kiss and a murmured, "If you need me, I will come."

She cupped his cheeks. "Ditto!" She winked when he blustered.

The mop fitted between her legs, he arched a brow. She blushed because she didn't need to read his mind to know where it went.

Marjorie huffed, "If you're done making googly eyes, can we go?"

They took to the sky, not saying much, as they both had to pay attention to the magic that kept anyone looking to the sky from seeing them. While Clarabelle went with a classic mirror shield that reflected the sky around her to anyone looking, she noted Marjorie instead chose a bird illusion, a big dark crow. Interesting idea. It might be a better option for Dracin for daytime flights, because, no matter what Marjorie said, Clarabelle would be staying with him.

The Barn owned by Theodore's clan turned out to be in the midst of an overgrown farm field, the exterior wooden planks of it a faded gray from the elements, with more recent patches to repair weak spots standing out in stark contrast. They didn't need to peek inside to smell the stench of death and decay. Ferals weren't known to be fastidious like their vampire makers. Something in them lost what humanity they used to have and turned them into blood-hungry beasts.

"You keep watch on the far side for any that might try to escape," Marjorie declared, lifting her hands to ignite.

"Where are they going to go?" The bright sunshine would roast any feral that tried to run.

"Are you going to be contrary about everything I say?" her coven leader growled.

Rather than reply with more sass, Clarabelle stomped to the other side of the barn. She tapped her foot while the structure went up in flames, the black smoke a beacon that would draw firefighters. They'd be gone before their arrival.

No one screamed or tried to flee the inferno, and so they took to the sky once more, with Clarabelle sliding close enough to try and speak. "I thought you brought a team."

"I did."

"Then how come they weren't in that field?"

"Because the barn didn't have any exits, so I sent them to watch over the sewer nest. While we've pinpointed the location, the many tunnels will make it harder to contain the ferals within for culling, not to mention we won't be able to just set the place on fire with all the moisture and concrete."

"What's the real reason you didn't want me bringing Dracin? We both know I could have conjured a cloud for us to travel in."

"Because a single moving cloud isn't strange at all."

"People would have remarked on it and gone on with their day," her hot retort. "Why are you so convinced he's bad?"

"Know any good vampires?"

"Not yet. But I have known some bad witches. Met

one yesterday who thought nothing of me being put in a cage, collared from my magic, and then stealing it from me."

"A rarity rather than the norm," Marjorie scoffed.

"Given neither of us met dragons before, couldn't the same be said of Dracin?"

"Hoping he's a rarity could see you dead."

"Then that would be my own fault. I don't know why you're being so obstinate about this," Clarabelle argued. "He's been nothing but kind to me. Risking himself for me."

"I don't want to see you hurt. Best to end it before that happens. I'm just looking out for you."

A sudden insight hit. and she blurted out, "You fell in love with a non-witch, didn't you?"

For a second, Marjorie didn't reply. When she did, she had a flat tone. "There was a man I met when I was much younger. A selkie, who rescued me from a boating accident. We became lovers, and he wanted me to become his wife."

"But you said no?"

"Actually, I said yes, without thinking because I thought I was in love. But a selkie can't live on land full time, although he tried. Tried until the lack of water drove him mad." She went silent before adding softly, "He tried to take me to his home at the bottom of a bay. I almost drowned. Had to kill him to escape and save myself. For a while after, I wished I had because of the pain in my heart. You see, I, too, thought I could ignore the differences between us.

That love would conquer all. But love almost killed me."

"I'm sorry for what happened," her soft reply. "But my situation isn't like yours. For one, Dracin lives in a house. He has a job, and he participates in society."

"He's a dragon with needs you can't understand."

"And I'm a witch who will also have things he can't grasp. It's up to us to discuss and work through those issues."

"What if you can't? What if he, too, one day goes mad and hurts you?"

"If that ever happens, then you can say 'I told you so.' But you have to realize your bad experience doesn't automatically mean all mixed matings will fail."

"You're like a daughter to me, Clarabelle."

"I know, and I love you too, but you have to trust me."

"I do." Marjorie sighed. "I just hope you're not wrong."

The moment of understanding explained much, but Clarabelle didn't have time to fully delve into it, as they arrived at a rooftop, where Bessie waited for them.

Bessie provided a summary of what they'd done. "We've sealed as many tunnels and shafts as we could find in a half-mile radius around the nest. Grates leading to the outside are being watched where there is little traffic. However, there were too many for us to completely cover. Not to mention, some of them are busy with foot and vehicle traffic."

"Well, now that I'm here with Clarabelle, we can provide extra eyes."

Clarabelle glanced to the sky, the blue still vivid, but a sharp wind from the west had her glancing to see clouds racing in. "We need to move fast before it gets dark enough for them to move."

Marjorie took a post at a busy alley, while Clarabelle got to keep an eye on the street directly above the nest. Unlikely they'd choose to boil out into the open, but desperation might force them out.

When the magical bomb unleashed underfoot, Clarabelle felt more than saw the result. The pavement undulated ever so slightly, but not enough to bother the steady stream of cars. Then smoke emerged, foul and dark, which had some of the pedestrians covering their faces and complaining. A bus rolled to a stop over the spewing grate, the driver putting on his hazards before emerging and running into a sandwich shop.

Clarabelle couldn't crouch to watch the sewer grate without looking odd, but she could bend over and tie her shoe. It would have helped if people didn't keep blocking her view. It wasn't as if she expected a feral to suddenly pop out, though. Where would it go? The bus would only provide temporary cover.

Just as she rose, her shoe tied so well it might never come off again, she saw something. A movement under the bus. Before she could get closer for a crouched peek, the driver hopped back in, sandwich in hand, along with a coffee. As he drove off, the whiff of burning flesh had her cursing.

She took after the bus on foot, spare phone borrowed from Marjorie—since Dracin informed that her own phone had been destroyed—allowing her to text, *Following a bus. Might have a feral clinging to the undercarriage.*

Marjorie replied: *K.*

Thankfully traffic kept the bus from moving fast. She had almost caught up to the vehicle at the next light when it started moving. She paused her panting butt for a second, cursing the fact she couldn't magic her shoes to fly when she realized the grate the bus had been stopped over was moved to the side, a smear of something gross along its edge.

As she went to text Marjorie to tell her she'd be going into the sewers to follow, someone bumped into her and knocked her phone onto the road, where it got promptly run over.

Dammit.

She hesitated only a second before throwing a quick cloak around herself so that no one would notice the woman who jumped into the hole. Hopefully she wouldn't be too long. An injured feral should be easy to track.

Wrong.

16

Belle left, and Dracin worried she wouldn't return. Not because of the vampires they hunted. Belle could handle those. It was the head witch, Marjorie, that concerned him. He just knew she'd be getting in Belle's ear, nattering about how they shouldn't be together. Bad-mouthing his kind.

Maybe she spoke the truth. After all, the only other dragon he ever encountered tried to kill him. Yet, until the vampires, Dracin had never killed anything other than wild animals. Sure, he'd been in fights, the kind that used fists and where all parties walked away with bruised bodies and egos. He could hold his own if shoved, but he wasn't a killer, and really, did vampires even count?

Even if he were, he would never harm Belle.

But would that matter? The coven leader seemed bound and determined to separate them. Who was to say she wouldn't use magic to convince Belle?

Mate come back. His dragon seemed rather clear on that point, but he couldn't stem the nagging feeling something was amiss.

Late afternoon, the sky turned dark. Storm clouds moved in, bringing deep shadows to the land. He found himself going around the house, looking out windows, checking the locks, checking his guns. Despite the current laws, he kept them loaded. He didn't have kids to worry about playing with them, just himself and a fear that one day his secret would be exposed. He'd rather go out in a blaze of bullets than waste away as a prisoner to science.

On his second outside circuit around his house, he heard the rumble of an engine. A familiar rumble that turned into his truck, kicking up dust and stone as it came to a sliding halt in his driveway.

Long strides brought him close enough to greet, only to scowl as Marjorie, not Belle, exited the vehicle. "You."

"Lovely to see you again," she replied just as sarcastically.

"Where's Belle?"

"She's not here?" The witch frowned.

"Is she supposed to be?" he snapped rather than letting his panic unleash.

"She went chasing after a feral that escaped our net."

"Alone?" he bellowed.

"It was just one. She should be fine."

"Fine and yet you don't know where she is," he pointed out with a glower.

"Calm your ass down, reptile. You'd know if she was dead."

"How do you figure?" He ignored the fact that Marjorie somehow figured out he wasn't a furry shifter.

Her lips turned down. "Because a true mate bond always knows."

Alive, his dragon confirmed.

"Why are you here if you're so convinced she's fine? She was supposed to be the one bringing back my truck."

The older witch chewed her lower lip. "I wanted to talk to you."

"About?" He crossed his arms.

"Clarabelle is very important to me. I don't want to see her hurt."

"Says the woman who left her alone to hunt a rabid vampire."

"Fighting monsters is easy. She's always been one of our best. But when it comes to men, you specifically, I'm afraid she's not as experienced. She doesn't seem to grasp the difficulties a mating with a non-witch will bring."

He arched a brow. "Such as?"

"She'll lose her position."

"Ah yes, because who she's fucking really affects her job performance," he drawled.

"Your attitude isn't helping," the witch snapped.

"My attitude? Listen, lady, you're the one who came here spouting how I'm some kind of murdering monster. Insulting me in my own home. Telling me I'm not good enough for Belle. And maybe I'm not. I'm certainly not rich. I'm a blue-collar kind of guy. But I'm also hard-working and loyal."

"The man part of you is. What of the dragon?"

"The dragon says you're annoying."

"It speaks to you?" she queried.

"That surprises you?"

"I guess I've not fully realized the complex nature of the bond between man and beast. I'd always assumed shifting was just about changing shape."

"It's a part of me," Dracin corrected. "I know what it thinks and feels. And it goes both ways."

"Fine, but if either side of you harms Clarabelle, I'll kill you," she threatened, daring to shake her finger at him in his own driveway.

"One, I never would, and if by some fluke I did, you wouldn't have to act because I'd make sure I never could again." With that, he was done talking. He needed to find Belle. He shifted, not caring if his clothes tore, not giving a fuck that the witch gaped as he went from man to dragon.

With a mighty shove of his legs, he pushed himself into the sky, as high as he dared to go with the clouds and their angry rumble of thunder. Not that he worried about lightning. He'd always had an affinity for storms. This high overhead, he could see for miles around, his vision sharper than an eagle's. Every tiny movement on the ground a thing to laser-focus on and identify.

The squirrel leaping from branch to branch.

The pair of blue jays squawking as they found cover before the storm.

On the other side of the forest hiding his place from sight, a car parked on the shoulder of the road, its trunk open. A few flaps of his wings gave him a better angle to see through the driver's side window and the body slumped over the wheel.

Heart attack? But what of the open cargo?

"Die, foul creature." The cry came from Marjorie, and he spun midair to see her on the ground by his truck, confronting a partially burned husk.

Theodore lived!

No for long. As he headed back for his place, he noticed the vampire glowed as if his entire body were wrapped in magic.

A magical shield as it turned out, given how it bounced Marjorie's attack. The ricocheting ball of fire she tossed came zooming back, and the witch only narrowly dodged it.

The half-baked vampire uttered a breathy chuckle, his voice a harsh rasp. "Fool me once, shame on me. You can't harm me with your magic. I've protected myself since the attack. Where is the dragon and his witch?"

"Not here." Marjorie lifted her chin.

"Tell me where?"

"I don't think so." She flung out her hand, aiming

for the ground under his feet, which rumbled and heaved, but the vampire floated above it.

"Your magic can't harm me. Not while the blood of the pack runs through my veins. I knew their immunity to witch magic would come in handy one day. Pity they taste so bad."

"It won't make you immune forever," Marjorie retorted.

"Long enough for you to die." Theodore lunged, and she wasn't quick enough to escape the clawed and burnt fingers that gripped her by the throat.

Fluttering overhead and watching, Dracin could have let Marjorie die. After all, she wanted Belle to leave him. Wanted to take his mate. Keep them apart.

If Marjorie were gone, he'd have no one to worry about.

Only, he knew Belle wouldn't approve, and what she thought of him meant more than anything.

Without any bugle of warning, he swooped down from the sky, arrowing in on the vampire intent on making the witch his victim. Theodore's burnt body oozed from its injuries, his fangs extending in preparation for his next meal. The witch.

Only at the last moment did Theodore think to look up. His bloodshot eyes widened as he saw the gaping jaw coming for him.

Crunch.

While usually a fan of barbecued meat, Dracin spat out the head. *Burnt rotted meat. Blech*. He spat a few times to get the foul taste out.

Marjorie stood there blinking at him before pinching her lips and saying a reluctant, "Thank you."

She should thank him, because his dragon wanted to eat her something fierce but Dracin firmly told it no.

It helped that he sensed a presence nearby.

Belle had returned.

17

CLARABELLE TRACKED THE ESCAPING VAMPIRE FOR HOURS before finally giving up. She'd lost its trail when it emerged from the sewer by a grocery store parking lot. She could only assume it had hitched a ride in someone's car.

With no way to track it, she decided to head back to Dracin, the broom she filched from the hardware store —using a spell to convince the clerk she'd paid—a stylish thing with a thick wooden handle and old-school straw bristles, none of that plasticky vinyl crap so popular these days.

With her personal phone destroyed and the spare run over, she'd have to borrow Dracin's to let Marjorie know at least one feral had escaped. Hopefully she wouldn't have to argue again with her mentor.

The story about the selkie had helped her understand Marjorie's concern, but at the same time, Clarabelle wouldn't let her tragedy interfere with her happiness. Would it be hard to be cast out from the coven?

Yes.

But at the same time, it didn't mean she had to stop being a witch. She could always pray to the Dark Lord as an independent. And if he rejected her, too, there were others who would welcome a witch with her level of power.

As she neared Dracin's place, she noticed the car on the road nearby with its trunk open. She swooped down, low enough to see the body slumped within, the neck torn out.

A chill settled in her bones.

This wasn't the work of a dumb feral. She took to the sky again and saw her dragon, hovering in the distance, watching events unfolding on the ground. She cast a spell to hear, her fear turning into hard reality as she realized Theodore had survived—and was going to kill Marjorie.

She'd never make it in time, but before she could yell at Dracin to act, he dove. Dove and ended the threat to Marjorie. Ended the vampire who'd killed his father. Ended the reign of terror in this city.

For a moment, she worried he'd also end the one person who seemed determined to ruin their happiness.

He could have taken Marjorie out in that moment too. Clarabelle would have even understood why.

But he didn't.

He shifted back into his man shape and said, "You're welcome."

In that moment, she saw just how much he loved her. He loved her enough to let Marjorie live, even though she wanted to break them apart.

Clarabelle swooped in and landed, smoothly dismounting her broom as she strode for Marjorie. "I'd say you owe Dracin more than thanks. How about an apology for saying all dragons are evil?"

For once, the older woman looked chagrinned. "It's what I was told. What the history books—"

"Fuck the books," her harsh reply. "Dracin isn't a monster. He's a man. My man. My lover. And he just saved your life. That has to mean something."

Dracin slid an arm around her and murmured, "It's okay. I didn't save her because I expected anything in return."

"But you should. We are not Wiccans or Christians who do things out of charity. We are the Dark Lord's witches. We can and do expect payment when someone does us a favor, and there is no bigger one than saving a life. So?" She glared at her coven leader.

Marjorie pressed her lips and nodded. "I will ensure you aren't demoted."

"Not good enough," Clarabelle stated. "I want the coven to accept my mating with Dracin."

"That won't be easy. You can't expect them to simply agree," Marjorie argued.

"Then convince them."

"I might be able to, if"—Marjorie eyed Dracin—

"he agrees to a few interviews to show the others he's not a menace."

"Interviews, yes, but no magic, no samples, no trying to bind him with a curse," she negotiated right back.

"Agreed." They shook on it, the magic binding the promise while Dracin looked on with confusion.

"What just happened?" he asked.

"Congratulations. You're now officially mated in the eyes of the coven and, as such, will enjoy its protection," a sour Marjorie answered.

"I don't need protecting," a bristling naked Dracin said.

"It's a good thing," Clarabelle soothed.

"Listen to her. You'll need this because not everyone will be as nice as me about it," Marjorie groused.

"Nice?" he snorted.

"Nice only to a certain point. Hurt her, and I will hunt you down and make you wish you'd never been born." With that threat, Marjorie stalked off, stealing Clarabelle's new ride to take off into the storming sky.

"Well, that was fun," he remarked.

Her turn to snort. "She must like you. She's usually not so nice." She flicked her fingers, and the vampire corpse on the ground ignited. "Thank you for not letting her die."

"Don't thank me. I wanted to let him eat her," he grumbled. "But I knew you wouldn't like it."

"And that makes you a better person than me. I

probably would have let him bite her before I stepped in," her evil reply.

To which he chuckled and dragged her close. "I'm glad you're safe, Belle."

"I'll always come back to you, my dragon."

As thunder rumbled, his lips crushed hers, devouring her in a passionate kiss that made her burn for more. He was already naked. It took only moments for her to shed her sewer-traipsing garments. They stood outside, naked, while lightning flashed and the world rumbled.

Or was it him making her quake?

His hand delved between her thighs, the tips of his fingers teasing her clit before parting her nether lips to find her wet and ready.

"Let's go inside," he murmured against her mouth as the first patter of raindrops hit their hot skin.

"Let's not. I like a good storm," she said, lifting her leg to open herself to him.

His hands grabbed her around the waist for a lift, his strength holding her aloft as she grabbed hold of his big cock, rubbing the tip of it against her. She guided his shaft into her sex, clenching in excitement because she knew now what to expect.

He stretched her so perfectly. Filled her so deeply. With his hands cupping her ass, he bounced her, hitting her sweet spot inside, making her breath hitch.

Faster and faster they moved amidst the wildness of the storm. Their lips meshed, their bodies locked, their passion intertwined.

Her fingers dug into the thick muscles of his shoulder as her pleasure peaked.

"Belle." He sighed her name as he continued to piston, his flesh slapping into hers with a savagery that matched the storm. Each stroke making her coil tighter and tighter. What sent her over the edge? When he nipped her. The pinch made her come hard, and she screamed, not that it could be heard amidst the thunder, a non-stop clash that shook the very foundation of the world.

When she finally stopped shaking, she noticed the pounding rain and laughed.

"What's so funny?" he asked.

"I do believe this storm is the Devil's way of saying he approves."

"What makes you say that?"

"Because he knows Marjorie hates flying in the rain."

They were still laughing when they entered the house. Their home.

For now.

She had a feeling she'd still be doing the Devil's work, with her new mate.

EPILOGUE

Months later...

"Your eggs are almost ready," Dracin announced, cooking bravely in the buff. She'd never risk her tender skin with spattering bacon grease. But her dragon mate? He strutted around the kitchen without a care, dick swinging, making her food. Hopefully she could eat it. She'd been feeling off the last few days. Blame the stress of everything going on. Despite Marjorie's promise, Clarabelle had been slightly worried.

For nothing as it turned out.

The coven didn't fire Clarabelle, but they also didn't want her hanging around with her dragon mate. Apparently, they worried if it became common knowledge that a witch and shifter could make dragon babies together, more might try and intentionally do so. Never mind the fact that only true-mated couples could procreate without difficulty. They also worried Dracin might be an anomaly and that future dragon babies would be the rampaging kind of old.

Whatever. She didn't like constantly having to report to the coven, anyway. She'd rather have her freedom to roam. With Dracin to love, she could—

She lurched from her chair and barely made it to the small bathroom off the kitchen. The tea she'd been sipping came up and, with that, everything she'd eaten in her entire life. Or so it felt.

By the time she was done heaving, she trembled and Dracin held back her hair.

"My poor Belle," he murmured. "Let's get you to bed so you can sleep this off."

"This won't go away with a nap." She leaned back into his solid strength and murmured, "And I'm not sick, just pregnant."

He stiffened then uttered a bugling cry that almost rendered her deaf before swooping her into his arms and crushing her.

Then practically shoved her from him, looking appalled. "Did I crush it?" He glanced down at her flat belly.

She snorted. "You idiot. I'm fine. We can hug. Have sex. I'll even be able to eat once I whip up an antinausea tea."

"But how?" He glanced at her with confusion. "I thought I was sterile?"

A conclusion drawn after one of the biology-oriented witches examined him and declared that the special conditions for a dragon's own conception meant that they wouldn't be able to make babies of their own.

Clarabelle shrugged and smiled. "Guess not. Wonder if the child will take after you or me."

His eyes widened. "Fuck me, it better be like you. I was a bit of a shit."

Her laughter spilled as she squeezed his hand. "And you think I was any better?"

He tucked her to his chest murmuring, "I love you, Belle."

"I love you more, my fierce dragon."

Together they would face the world that would have kept them apart and maybe help others to realize that love could transcend all boundaries.

And if not, she'd send them to Hell and let her Dark Lord sort them out.

THE END of the story was inspired by Broomstick Breakdown. *I had so many people ask about Dracin and Clarabelle that I finally had to find out how their love story began. But now I wonder, is there someone else in this world of claws, furs, and fangs that needs to find love?*

www.ingramcontent.com/pod-product-compliance
Lightning Source LLC
LaVergne TN
LVHW031540060526
838200LV00056B/4586